Volume One

These stories are dedicated to all the people who said I never would.

To my family who always believed I could.

And the people who never got to see this dream become reality.

-Willow Diedian

Volume One

Volume One

Table of Contents

Book One: Daemon Rising

Prelude   Pg. 6

Chapter One   Pg. 15

Chapter Two   Pg. 27

Chapter Three   Pg. 46

Chapter Four   Pg. 57

Chapter Five   Pg. 82

Chapter Six   Pg. 99

Chapter Seven   Pg. 117

Chapter Eight   Pg. 137

Chapter Nine   Pg. 157

Book Two: Pack Beginnings

Volume One

Prelude	Pg. 170
Chapter One	Pg. 183
Chapter Two	Pg. 195
Chapter Three	Pg. 218
Chapter Four	Pg. 231
Chapter Five	Pg. 254
Chapter Six	Pg. 265
Chapter Seven	Pg. 275
Chapter Eight	Pg. 284
Chapter Nine	Pg. 292

Book Three: Family Bonds

Prelude	Pg. 309
Chapter One	Pg. 319
Chapter Two	Pg. 332
Chapter Three	Pg. 343

Volume One

Chapter Four   Pg. 355

Chapter Five   Pg. 362

Chapter Six   Pg. 372

Artharthian Lore   Pg. 385

Volume One

Volume One

Prelude

The wind howled outside and a moonless night darkened all the land about the castle that sat upon the mist swept highland moors of Athartha. Inside the weathered castle walls a tall handsome man paced in front of a heavy iron bound door listening to the shuddering heartbeat of his mate, Lady Shadow, within. He could hear also the frantic whispering of the servants as they attended to her needs as her labor drew nigh. The man growled to himself as he listened to the pained breathing of Shadow.

There was nothing he could do for her; he had already gathered within his walls the best midwife and physician the Immortal world had to offer. Lord Albert Van Sewdan was the Immortal Royal physician and the only man, Prince Vladimir would trust to deliver his child or care for Shadow during this difficult process of Immortal child birth. He could only hope she would pull through this birthing safely, her and the child. This was by no means easy for him; he was in agony not knowing whether or not

Volume One

Shadow was going to make it, whether or not their child was going to make it. The loss of his mate, the woman who made his life worth living would be devastating enough, but to lose his child in the same fell swoop that would be unbearable. A servant stepped out of the room with a flushed face to report to him. None of the servants knew with certainty that Lady Shadow was his mate, and this child was his child.

Though if they suspected such they wisely kept such thoughts to themselves. Otherwise to them Lady Shadow was just merely his dear childhood friend, whom had come to call unexpectedly in the night and then gone into labor from the strenuous journey she had undergone to bring her to his estate.
"The Lady is doing well; Lord Albert thinks the child will come soon." The servant reported breathlessly. The man nodded curtly and resumed his relentless pacing, wringing his large and roughly calloused hands nervously.

He had caught a glimpse of Shadow when the door had opened. Her face was tired and flushed with effort, her raven dark hair damp with sweat. For a split second her dark eyes had met his and they had glowed green in the dim candle light reminding him of what she was and how forbidden it was for them to be together. Let alone how dangerous it was for them and the child they had created together. He smiled grimly baring long fangs in the dim light of the torch sconces that lined the hall. Another servant approached him from down the hall. The man hissed in distaste at yet another interruption but listened to the servant nonetheless, his patience wearing thin with the lads' stammered mutterings in his ear. "Prince Vladimir, a letter has arrived for you from your father." The servant whimpered into his ear holding out the parchment envelope sealed with a crimson wax seal with the Immortal Royal coat of arms sealed into it. The man took the letter and pocketed it. He would read it later; at the moment he had far more pressing concerns to deal with now. The servant bowed and withdrew hurrying away.

    Vladimir continued to pace worriedly waiting anxiously; fervently listening for any change in the frantic beating of Shadow's heart or the heartbeat of his child with his keen ears, though he doubted he could have heard anything else over the drumming of his own anxious heart. He wished he had a strong drink in his hand to ease his nerves and was thinking of calling a servant to fetch him some when there was a sudden fierce wailing, the wailing of a newborn child drowning out nearly all other sound.

    The sound of it stopped Vladimir dead in his tracks, he listened to it for a bit longer his hand hesitating on the handle of the door. Slowly the door was opened and the portly physician Albert, who had been until that moment attending to Shadow ushered him into the room. Vladimir went to stand by Shadow numbly looking down at the small bundle in her arms as she rested against the head board of the bed.

"Tis a boy my Lord, you have a son." She said lightly holding the bundle out for him to see, like she was scared of how he was going to react to the babe.

After all she had only very recently told him of her pregnancy and through a letter at that, few weeks before showing up on his doorstep to explain herself in person because of his stupid demand that she explain herself to him and going into labor due to the stress of the arduous journey she had undergone. Vladimir took the infant slowly with all the reverence in the world he could muster. He was a father, this was his son there was no denying it, not now that he could see such a strong resemblance to himself in the babe.

A slow smile broke on his face as he held his son; he leaned over and kissed Shadow softly. Reiterating what she had said softly. "We, we have a son my Lady." Vladimir looked down on his son's sleeping face and smiled again. But his happiness was short lived as it dawned upon him, the dangers that surrounded their son should anyone realize what he was and they would be hard pressed not to when he grew older and began feeding, if he began feeding as Vladimir did. What were they going to do? The child could not live with him, and he surely could not visit the child, not as his father. Not without risking his own father finding out about the child and killing both his mate and the child.

This love, it was forbidden, their son in the eyes of Vladimir's father and the majority of the Courts and common Immortals was an abomination. He would not be allowed to live. If it was ever to be found out that this child was of his flesh and blood and the child was sure to grow to be more akin to him in appearance as he grew older, save for that shock of ebony hair. If any of the Immortals in the court found out about this child and told his father before this child was old enough to stand on his own two feet. That would be the end of this precious life, no his very existence was already his death warrant. Vladimir knew it in his heart; his father would not suffer his son to live, not for long. He stroked the face of his son lovingly as these torturous thoughts assailed him.

His mate could keep his son safe that was for sure at least until his son could stand on his own, her pack would do nothing to betray her, not openly at least. But for his son's safety, neither of them could not remain here, they had already caused quite a commotion by coming here. Vladimir knew why she had come; she felt safe here with him and he had asked her, demanded that she explain things to him properly. Because until she stood on his doorstep he had not believed a word that she had written. Shadow trusted him to keep his staff from blabbing their secret and so far no one had, though there were more than a few flighty rumors about him, her, and their affairs floating about the castle.

But with this, the birth of their son, and the speculation it would soon bring, was too big to trust scullery maids to keep quiet about. He had to send her away; Vladimir felt the tears streaking down his face as he pressed his son back into his mate's arms.

"What are you going to name him Mo grá?" *my love*. He asked lightly in Shadow's native tongue the language of the Northern isles of Athartha, trying not to choke on the words as he said them. She smiled up at him with a beautifully innocent smile.

Her eyes though said she had the same thoughts as him, that she had come to the same decision, and they were sad, full of longing. "Vladimir is a strong name to pass from father to son." She said softly full of love, Vladimir leaned down to kiss her a final time. "B'fhéidir go mbeidh sé a thabhairt dó do neart…" she whispered to him as he left the room. *Maybe it will give him your strength.* Vladimir slumped against the closed door and struggled to compose himself as her words echoed in his ears. He was glad that his son would at least have his name if he could have nothing else from him for the time being at least, tears streaked down his face and Vladimir grimaced and wiped them away angrily. How he wished he could right the wrongs of the Immortal Nations right then! Vladimir wanted to wash away all of the hate and the pain that would follow his son, banishing away all of the corruption in the world with his tears and his fury.

But slowly his anger faded, Vladimir was a man of many talents, talking was one of them, persuading was one of them; he was a man of vision. But he was not a man steel and violence. Vladimir hated himself for that, and how he had won the heart of one of the strongest and vicious wolves in the Northern Woods of Athartha without fighting half the men in her pack for her hand he did not know. Straightening himself Vladimir strode down the hall and opened the letter in his pocket and sighed at the contents. His father demanded his presence at a potential partnership meeting. He growled and crumpled the letter in his fist before throwing it into the nearest fireplace and watched as it went up in flames.

    There was nothing he wanted to do more than go back to Shadow and hold her tight, but he could not, he would not. He had to leave her. For both their sakes he had to pretend that she was nothing more than a guest in his home. She would be gone soon enough, taking his son with her.

Volume One

Chapter One

Looking into a pool of water Vladimir surveyed his ebony eyes and hair, before looking out over the forest his ebony eyes searching for his mother, young Vladimir whined under his breath. He could feel many unfriendly eyes on him, and it was making him itch, his skin was practically crawling with the anticipation of what he knew was to come; he was on a little rise above the village in which they lived. His mother had left early in the morning to hunt with some of the other members of the pack but it was near dark now, the hunting party should have been back by now, this was not normal for his mother.

Unlike him his mother, Shadow was welcome in the pack; the pack accepted her because she was the Alpha, her word was law and she was respected, loved even. But they did not accept him, and he knew why, it was no secret that he was a mongrel; he was not entirely lycanthropic like the rest of the pack. His mother admitted it openly, proudly, his father was not a werewolf like her, his father, as the pack led him constantly to believe was just a common lowly Vampire. Vladimir snarled, coming to a standing position, his posture defensive, as the menacing feeling grew and took the shape of a group of lads larger and stronger looking than him.

"Look here boy's the mongrel's on his own again, where is your mother mongrel?" the leader asked as he shoved Vladimir to the ground. Vladimir bared his fangs eyes flashing dangerously in the light of the dying sun.

"You know perfectly well where she is." Vladimir growled standing back up and dusting off his breeches and chest which was bared to the cool breeze that was coming from the East through the trees.

The leader of the gang laid hands on him again trying to shove him back to the ground. Vladimir snarled raising his lip over his teeth threateningly. The youth slugged him in response, his fist smacking into Vladimir's jaw and knocking him to the ground where he stayed fighting the change, heat and pain washing down his spine as his voice rising in the air in a menacing snarl.

"And are you going to do about it you filthy mongrel? There is ten of us and one of you..." the youth never got the rest of his sentence out because Vladimir had risen and was on him, the rest of his sentence resounded as a terrified shriek that split the air.

Vladimir was all ripping claws, snarling fangs, and roaring fury his form had shifted as he went through the air at the lad and he had already taken a half form by the time the third blow fell. Vladimir was a whirlwind of snarling fury striking at anything that moved. The air was filled with panicked shrieking and the ground was quickly becoming slick with blood and mud. Three of the boys fled bleeding profusely from long ragged wounds in their arms and shoulders.

Vladimir saw only red his instincts urged on by the fading screams of his victims he wanted to hurt, to maim, to shred, to break, to tear these weaker opponents apart like they would have done to him. He did not hear the adults yelling as they ran up the hill towards the fight, he heard only the snarls of his own voice in his ears, and felt only his fangs and claws rending flesh. More of the boys fled in terror of him but Vladimir had a hold on the leader of the gang, the lad that had caused him so much grief. His fangs sunk deep into the lad's shoulder, the taste of blood in his mouth raising in him an unspeakable desire in him, a hunger that he *had* to satisfy.

    Large rough hands seized him, pulling hard at the loose folds of his skin, clubbing at his ears as someone called his name and strong hands tried to pry his jaws apart but only added to the taste of blood in his mouth as they shredded their hands on his teeth, Vladimir instinctively tightened his grip and snarled. This was his *kill*. His instincts and the hunger had him now, the pain made Vladimir whimper but he could not let go. It was like he was a starved man whom had finally found the food he'd been missing all his life.

    The adults could not pry him off the lad that had terrorized him for the better part of his life, they could not even reason with him. Taken by his thirst, his hunger and his rage, Vladimir could not be reasoned with.

"Someone get this demon off my son!" A terrified female voice cried "he's killing him!" there was a long pause and a cool and familiar voice spoke from not far off.

"If your son would just leave him alone maybe this would not have happened." Vladimir looked up his vision clearing as he slowly recognized that voice that was his mother's voice. She knelt before him and smiled gently. "Vladimir you can let go now, take your full shape and go I will find you when I have taken care of this." Her voice was soft when she spoke with him, Vladimir felt his bones grinding together as his form settled into the full form of a wolf and let go of the boy he had been feeding on.

No one dared to touch him further, though they did glare at him and growl in his direction as he made his way through the throng of adults. They would not dare to touch him, not in the presence of his mother so Vladimir walked away. Settling on the crest of the hill where he had been before the lads had come to bother him. He looked down on the scene unfolding below him with his head on his paws.

A few hours later when the boy had been removed from sight Vladimir sat up as his mother came up the hill with a fresh pair of breeches. She stroked his face from nose to the crown of his head and rubbed behind his ears soothingly.
"The boy is dead Vladimir." She said softly as she pet him. Vladimir leaned against his mother and whined. Not out of guilt for what he'd done, but for the sadness his mother felt. He knew she had a pack to run, so even if that bastard had deserved it. His mother still had to punish him for taking a life.

She made a shushing motion and sat next to him as mournful howls echoed through the village below. Vladimir felt no pity, no sadness for what he had done; he had defended himself against a gang of thugs. Thugs that would have killed him if they had been allowed to and they would have. The other members of the pack that had come to their aid would never have come to

Vladimir's. His mother knew this fact, the pack knew this fact. It did not make a difference though, he was an outcast in the pack, and there would be hell to pay for what he had done despite what his mother's position was within the pack, more accurately for her position in the pack.

His mother stroked his face again, running her hands through his fur as she started to speak again, her voice sorrowful and serious.

"There is only one way I can protect you from this, the Trial of the shamed." Vladimir flinched and bowed his head. The Trail of the Shamed was not to be taken lightly. The offender was to complete ten tasks, Ten Trials mandated by traditional pack law. Vladimir would be the youngest participant in the trials, as he had barely reached the tender age of ten. His mother left the breeches next to him on the hilltop and descended into the village presumably to talk to the deceased boy's family about the Trail of the Shamed.

After having watched his mother descend the hill, Vladimir gathered the breeches into his mouth and descended the other side of the hill. Making his way carefully back to the cabin that he and his mother shared on the edge of the village. He paused as he reached the cabin, feeling ill at ease with the people gathered before the porch. There was a group of young men, cubs almost ready to become full-fledged members of the pack. And Vladimir recognized them to be led by the elder brother of the youth he had just killed. He knew what this was and he was determined to fight tooth and claw to the last.

    Shifting to stand before the cubs Vladimir pulled on his breeches, since he had been in his wolf form on his way home when he had run into them. That form had many advantages when hunting and fighting as a pack member. But being on your own and fighting a group of people it placed you in a bit of a disadvantage. Or so Vladimir had learned previously in another fight. Vladimir held his hands out to the sides he did not want any more trouble this night. He felt wired and energized when he should have felt tired and weary from his previous battle. It was like he was on some weird high. Like he had eaten havoar leaf and quite a bit of it, havoar was a plant that like aconite affected Immortals in large quantities or if it was prepared in certain ways.

    Not wanting to be pointed out as the aggressor in this conflict. Vladimir waited for the cubs to make the first move, when they did he ripped into them with all he had, keeping his cool was not Vladimir's strong suite and he soon lost all his composure and it devolved into an all for nothing brawl. Vladimir stayed standing under a hail of claws and fists for maybe two minutes three max before he was on his back fighting for his life, but he never once cried out for help or begged for mercy.

    Groaning Vladimir tried to lift his head. He was deep in the woods far from the village, after surveying his surroundings for a moment longer. Vladimir knew where he was, and it was going to be hell getting back to the village. The older cubs had beaten him within an inch of his life then dragged him out to the roaring waterfall twenty miles north of the village. Every cub knew where the falls were, because they were forbidden from ever going there. They were forbidden because of the tainted water, a fair bit of aconite grows around the water fall, and when the flowers shed their petals. They landed in the pool of water at the foot of the waterfall. Making the water a deadly poison capable of killing an adult immortal, Vladimir was still a child.

    It was there the cubs had shaken Vladimir to consciousness before tossing him over the edge of the falls. He had not landed in the water; Vladimir plummeted the first ninety feet in a free fall, before his fall had been broken by the branches of several close standing trees that had been at the bottom of the cliff. Twenty feet and several broken tree limbs later Vladimir crashed to the bracken strewn forest floor, right next to a bunch of aconite.

    He did not know how he had survived, but he was alive if only barely, and healing. Vladimir could feel all of his broken bones grating together and knew that if he did not set them he would have to re-break them later so they could heal properly. Hissing with his pain Vladimir sat up and began tending to his wounds.

It took Vladimir three hours to set all the fractures he could; there was nothing he could do nothing to do about his ribs, or his jaw. But his left arm and his shin he could do something about those, after re-breaking them to ensure that they healed properly. He tore his breeches and used a few short sturdy branches to splint the fractured limbs. After a few more hours of rest he used a couple of straight branches that had fallen when he had crashed to the earth as crutches.

Once he was able to get a foot under him, Vladimir hobbled to his feet and began to shuffle his way home. He reached the village boundaries around dawn the next day where he collapsed from exhaustion, and was found by his mother's Beta, Stephan. The man was not gentle as he dragged Vladimir to the village square, and threw him down in front of his mother, declaring.

"Here is your wayward child Lady Shadow, looks like he took a wrong turn on the way home and got lost in the woods." He said as he walked away, Vladimir looked up at his mother and looked back at the man and snarled weakly. He rested his head in his mother's lap and let himself be taken into oblivion.

Chapter Two

Shaking Vladimir gasped as he rolled away from the bear. His back had been laid open by the things claws and the grizzled beast was leering over him snarling as hot blood gushed down his back. The Barrett family had agreed to the trails of shamed and as he was still a child the severity of the trials were somewhat lessened, as in the trials were taking place in the village under the supervision of his mother and that was the extent of it.

The first Trial of the Trial of the shamed was the Trial of Perseverance; he was not to harm the bear no matter what the bear did to him. To ensure that he would not simply just run out from the animals reach. The Barrett's had decreed he was to be locked in with the beast. After observing his little cell that he shared with the enraged bear, Vladimir had to admit the cage was decidedly small. There was very little room for him to maneuver or to escape. He was stuck in a small box, with an animal that would rather eat him than share space, and defending himself physically was not an option. He was stuck between a rock and a hard place. Literally.

Vladimir looked to his mother who was sitting in her wolf form, looking regal and defined like an ebony statue. He winced and sat up feeling the hot blood pouring down his back as he did so. From the corner of his eye he could see his mother flinch and hear her whine. The sound was soft and low. Her eyes looked pained. Vladimir growled and looked the bear in the eyes and snarled menacingly. He did not lay a hand on the creature, just issued it a challenge. Asserting his dominance with his voice alone. The bear snarled back and they settled to the ends of the cage to wait each other out.

He was in the cage with the bear from before dawn to well after dusk, and no matter what the bear did to him Vladimir did not retaliate. When he was let out of the cage the Barrett's looked very displeased at the fact he had survived. When Vladimir's mother came to collect him the Barrett's let their displeasure be heard.

"So that beast of yours can control himself from time to time, when he wants to." They said to his mother in very snobbish and disrespectful tones. Vladimir growled he would not tolerate that could not tolerate it. They could say anything about him, but insinuating that his mother had not raised him right. That was something he was not just going to let slide.

    Vladimir snarled and stepped forward snapping his head in a curt bow to them. His voice rising to the whole square, so that the entire village would hear him. As many of them had come to watch the spectacle. Vladimir hated it, hated them all of them, this hurt his mother far worse than it would ever hurt him. He could and would survive the Trials of Shame, but what it was putting his mother through was so much worse than anything he had to endure.

"I will not harm an innocent creature that has done nothing to deserve my wrath save for food as my mother has taught me." Vladimir growled angrily. "Your son knew what he was doing when he provoked me into that fight, now I did not mean for him to die but that does not

change the fact that your son started the fight, and I finished it." The Barrett's looked at him shocked and stormed away in a huff.
"Your next trial takes place at dawn tomorrow." They called over their shoulders as they left.

    Vladimir growled as his mother prodded his wounds and filled them with foul smelling salve. She was humming an old Northern tune to him as she did so. Grabbing fresh linen she wrapped his wounds and bound them tightly. Vladimir fell asleep before the fire his body aching all over. When he woke it was a few hours before dawn and he slipped out of the house to the Barrett's to report in to commence with the trials. He was waiting for them on their porch when they woke in the morning.

    His second trial was the Trial of Humility, meant to teach him humility. For a full ten day period of time per adult member of the village he was to work like a serf for each adult member of the village, the members of the village did not leave it at that, naturally. Vladimir found himself at the beck and call of *every single* pack member in the community and if his mother tried to

Volume One

object the Barrett's would throw it in her face that he killed their son. It took months to serve to each of the adults and he was nearly done with all elder cubs before his mother put her foot down and call an end to it all. It was in the process of doing this trial that he started his third trial the Trial of Silence. In which Vladimir began three tasks, the endless hunt in which he provided meat for the Barrett's, the raising of the monument for his victim, and the carving of the Trial Horn which he would play once the Trials were over. All of which he did under an oath of silence which would end once the trials came to an end and the horn is played.

    Vladimir completed the Trial of Humility and began the Trial of Silence during that several month process. He then began the Trial of the Lost where he was rendered unconscious and placed in a random location in Athartha and expected to find his way home with no food, weapons, or money. The Trail of the Lost took Vladimir a few weeks since the pack was merciful and only placed him in a cave a league or so away from the village, but Vladimir was of the suspicion that they made that task so easy so they could send him on to the next trial. The Trial of the Black Throated Lily, this trial could very well have claimed Vladimir's life as it sent him across Athartha to the dangerous jungle lands of the Southern Packs in search of the rare Black Throated Lily; it took Vladimir a year to find this flower. When he returned he immediately faced the Trial of Wolves, he walked through a gauntlet of fully grown Lycanthropes accepting whatever abuse they gave him in his wolf form before presenting his belly to his Alpha, his mother.

    A few days later he built a roaring bon fire for the Trial of Fire, the bon fire was nine feet long and the flames jumped at least ten feet high big enough for a full grown man to walk through the heat was enough to make the entire village square swelter. But Vladimir had built the fire in such a way that he would have a long lasting fire tunnel to which he would walk back and forth through. Most whom faced this challenge only walked over blazing logs searing only their feet and legs. Vladimir had built his bon fire in such a manner to allow his entire body to feel the flames.

Brazen was used to describe him when the pack saw what he had built. Vladimir shrugged in response; he knew that this act could be considered Brazen. Vladimir stripped down and stood at the mouth of the fire tunnel knowing that the entire village was watching with anticipation, Vladimir stepped in. he walked with the flames licking his skin and the coals eating at his feet. The pain was horrendous but Vladimir did not cry out, he just lifted one foot and placed it in front of the other and walked on his eyes watering from the heat and the heat searing his eyes. He walked until he could not walk anymore and then he tried to crawl. When he was pulled from the fire he was hardly recognizable but he was alive.

Still recovering from his injuries from the Trial of the Fire Vladimir undertook the Trial of the Stones. This entailed carrying massive stones from one end of the village to the other for an entire month cycle. Shadow was beside herself with rage and worry. She had already called the Barrett's out twice to end this farce of the trials of the Shamed but both times Vladimir had interceded and ended the argument. He of course could not speak, but his mere presence was enough to silence his mother for the time being. Already Vladimir was becoming someone of note within the village.

It seemed since the trial of the fire opinions of him were slowly starting to change with the younger cubs, the children of the cubs that had thrown Vladimir off the cliff and the other smaller children treated Vladimir with awe and respect though Vladimir was hardly older than they were. When the Trial of the Stones was finished Vladimir was shackled to the monument he had built for Gable, the young cub he had killed. And he was shackled in such a manner that it was cruel. He was forced to kneel with his ankles shackled to the ground his wrists shackled behind him and the chain shackled to the monument was given no slack due to the chain around his neck bolted to the cobbles of the square below him, forcing him to bow his head.

He could theoretically break the chains but this was the Trial of Patience and each morning a fresh bowl of water and a fresh plate of food was brought out to him and left for the day just out of his reach. An adult Immortal can go about a month without eating anything, a young one can only go a week, which is why what the Barrett's did to Vladimir was very cruel, Shadow was called to settle a dispute with another pack after the first three days of Vladimir's ninth trial. She did not expect to be gone longer than another seven days.

Shadow instructed explicitly that Vladimir was to be released from the Trial of Patience after an Artharthian ten day week cycle had passed. She was delayed another two weeks. That was a whole month without food and water for such a young cub and when she returned to find Vladimir still chained to the monument he had painstakingly built for his victim almost a husk she flew into a rage and dragged the Barrett's out of their cabin thinking her cub was dead. She understood how the Barrett's felt, she too had lost cubs of her own before, but there was a difference between self-defense and murder.

When she had dragged the Barrett's back to the monument she pointed out her lifeless son and demanded an answer when suddenly Vladimir moved it was just a slight twitch, the rattling of his thin chest as he drew breath. Perhaps it was the fact that he was more than Lycanthrope that kept him alive, or the fact that his father was not a Vampire but an Ancient being predating both the younger Immortal races. Vladimir was certainly a mystery.

Shadow hurriedly pulled the key out of the Barrett's hand and unlocked the chains binding her son before pulling him into her lap. Wondering what in the world would restore him, he would certainly die at this rate. Shadow raised her wrist to her mouth and bit down letting the blood flow she, pressed her wrist to Vladimir's mouth. Slowly she watched as the life came back to her son. It took a lot of her strength but she gave him all she could without giving him all. Then she took him home.

It took three years for Vladimir to complete all ten of the Trials of the Shamed. At the end of the last trial the Barrett's approached him where he lay in his mother's lap with disdainful looks and that was only because he was still alive. He was unconscious from the thrashing he received from the were-badger they had set upon him as his final trial his mother glared up at them, it had been the Trial of Bravery, and it had been no more than an excuse to publicly execute him, only it had back fired. The Were-badger that had been placed in the ring with Vladimir had arrived in the village some weeks before the last task and had inquired why such a young cub was participating in the Trial of the Shamed.

The man had taken pity on Vladimir and had withheld the final blow, sparing Vladimir his life much to the Barrett's disappointment and allowing Vladimir to play his horn just as he faded into oblivion. The were-badger was off to the side watching the scene with a scowl; he had several nasty wounds of his own. As Vladimir had not gone down quietly. The were-badger stood and approached the Barrett couple; he looked from Vladimir to the Barrett's.

"I hope you two are pleased with yourselves, forcing a cub to fight for his life against a full grown man." the badger said coldly, the Barrett's growled.

"But he killed our son..." The badger snarled menacingly silencing their protest.

"It was a ten to one fight and from what I hear your son instigated it." The badger growled in return, "From what I hear your son constantly bullied this boy, tis no wonder he snapped, perhaps you should have taught your son some tolerance and respect and he would still be here this day." The badger growled and picked Vladimir up causing his mother to growl. He turned back to the Barrett's and spat at their feet in disgust.

"And then your eldest brags about how he and his friends taught this one a lesson by tossing him off the face of a cliff after beating him senseless in yet another ganged up fight of the strong against the weak." The were-badger growled at them staring them down until they stared at the dirt uncomfortably. "Then you subject this child to the Trial of the Shamed and he does whatever you ask of him without complaint, above and beyond what is asked of him even. While you degrade him and demean him knowing full well what your sons have done to him his entire life, this cub should not have suffered as he did." The were-badger growled at them angrily the disgust plain on his face, he spat again and said.

"It is the two of you whom should have had to endure the Trial of the shamed for allowing both your cubs to torture this cub in the manner that they did, for the manner in which you have tortured this cub." He snarled looking out at the entire village with angry eyes, many of the villagers eyes were cast down at the ground guiltily, because his words were not meant just for the Barrett's.

It was a loud verbal lashing meant for the entire village, and none dared confront the were-badger for what he said because it was the simple truth. He scoffed and turned to Vladimir's mother

"Come Lady Shadow lets treat your pup before he fades too far." The badger said softly, striding away towards the cottage that belonged to Vladimir and his mother.

Vladimir woke in pain, unable to move or do much of anything. He called out in his mother's native tongue.

"Máthair áit a bhfuil tú?" *mother where are you?* There was a gentle touch on his face and his mother leaned over him her scent enveloping him, tangy and spicy. She smiled and responded lightly.

"Tá mé anseo grá." *I am here love.* She stroked his face gently and he reached up to wipe at her tears. "You were asleep for a long time little one." She said slowly, Vladimir nodded and paused smelling a new scent, light but strangely heavy not to unlike his own, an oak and hemlock forest compared to Vladimir's pine and cedar scent. He tilted his head to the side trying to see whom it belonged to. There was a man standing off to the side of the door. He was a handsome man as far as Vladimir could tell; he seemed vaguely familiar as if he had seen him before.

Volume One

The man had coppery hair and strong build. The man nodded to Vladimir but remained where he was.

Vladimir groaned and tried to sit up but could not complete the action on his own; he had at least a dozen wounds in his stomach that prevented that. His mother helped him into a sitting position and spoon fed him some broth. The man watched them carefully but said nothing. Vladimir did not ask about the man figuring that his mother would introduce the man soon enough. His mother looked at the man and then to Vladimir with a sad look and said slowly.
"Vladimir this man here is your father, Vladimir the first." The man came forward and knelt by Vladimir's bedside. His mother continued her voice sorrowful. "He is not just your father though Vladimir, he is the Crown Prince." Vladimir felt like he had just been belted in the gut, so his father was not just some lowly common Immortal like the pack had lead him to believe? Like his mother had allowed him to believe, his father was Royalty? How could that

be? The Royals were not lycanthropic; they were not even Vampires though they survived off mortal blood like Vampires, no one knew what they were or what they could do.

So what did that make him? The man gave him a fanged smile and spoke in a reassuringly deep voice that calmed him answering the question that was glaringly obvious on his face. "You are perfect Vladimir." He said lightly, Vladimir looked at him carefully. He was apprehensive about this. This man had not been there to defend him against the pack, to defend his mother against the whispers that floated around that undermined her authority in the pack, hell this man did not even have the aura of a fighter, sure he was built very much so like one, and looked like he could wield the blade at his hip, but he was no warrior. This man, this man who was his father should have been there to protect him and his mother, this man should have been there but he had not been. Vladimir did not say anything though he just sat and watched, his eyes glowering with discontent.

Volume One

His mother and father withdrew to a more private part of the cottage to talk.

"Is he healing alright? I came as soon as I got your letter; I feared though that I would be too late." His father's voice said worriedly. His mother sighed and responded tiredly.

"Vladimir is healing fast, faster than either of us could ever hope to heal, particularly now since both of us have given him blood." She said softly, Vladimir strained to listen to the conversation. "What about your end, has your father found out?" there was a long pause before his father spoke again.

"My father suspects something; my visit here will not help." He said slowly. "He just does not know what I have deceived him of that is for sure." There was another long pause before Vladimir heard both his parents pacing.

"When Vladimir turns sixteen he will be a man by the pack laws, I will not be able to protect him then, but he will still be a child by your standards." His mother said carefully, "Vladimir needs you; he has needed you all along but until he turns sixteen he must remain here where the loyalty of my pack protects him." His father scoffed and growled.

"Good lot that the loyalty of your pack has been doing, my father knows that there is a powerful half-breed loose in the land, you have a leak my love and your pack is not too friendly with our son…" Vladimir the first trailed off before the silence deepened at the front of the cabin, his mother sighed. The front of the cabin was silent for a while. His parents muttering to themselves softly.

Vladimir relaxed into his pillows glad that they were done discussing him leaving though they were still muttering to each other too low for him to make out the conversation.

"Are you proposing that I come here on a regular basis?" his father asked slowly. There was a long silence before his mother answered.

"Do we have any other choice? Who else is going to take him into the human cities to feed? I certainly cannot and now that he has had a taste do you expect him to live off anything else?" she said calmly "He is more like you in that respect than we ever thought Vladimir."

There was another lengthy silence before his father spoke again.

"I cannot promise anything, but I will try to get away when I can." He said softly, there were steps coming towards Vladimir's section of the cottage and Vladimir quickly closed his eyes pretending to sleep as his parents came into the room.

"I would ask nothing more of you." His mother said softly as she came to Vladimir's bed side to stroke his face. Vladimir rolled into the touch and gradually drifted into sleep.

Chapter Three

Vladimir looked at the other cubs competing in the Trial of the Cubs and scoffed. He could easily best these pups in the trials. But the last six years had taught him caution if nothing else, many of these cubs would not mind slipping poison into his water or finding some other way to weaken or kill him. Not that they could do so, he had more than proven himself a dangerous opponent already and stronger than the norm for a cub of his age. The Task Masters looked at him with disdain as they painted his skin with the ceremonial paint; his paint was not the traditional crimson base layer the others were painted with, with the simple swirling designs.

No Vladimir's base layer was the deep emerald of sin, for the Trials of the Shamed and were blocked out across his body to show case the ten trials he had completed. As always he was an outcast here, but that was soon to change he would be going to live with his father soon as the trials were done or at least he hoped it was soon to change. He and his father had grown close in the last six years, as close as two complete strangers could get while trying to get the measure of each other. The Task Masters led the cubs to the circle and the trials began. The first trial was the Trial of Strength. A series of stones of varying sizes were rolled into a ring and lined up from smallest to largest, a dozen stones in all. The task was simple the cubs were to take the stones and lift them chest high and throw them as far as they could.

    Vladimir waited patiently at the outer rings for his name to be called and he entered the ring lifting the first few stones with ease and grace. As the stones grew larger the test of his strength grew and he found it increasingly difficult to lift the stones, but for him the task was not as difficult as it could have been or had seemed to be for the other cubs. But lift them all he did and send them sailing over the heads of astonished onlookers, even the largest of the stones went beyond the boundaries of the circle clearing the heads of the tightly packed ring of onlookers crashing down to earth behind them and shattering into pieces showering the closest of the onlookers with sharp fragments and chunks of rock. Vladimir dusted his palms off and walked out of the ring before the Task Masters could recover from their shock, before anyone could recover from their shock. The Task Masters had to catch up to him to paint his body with the second design of the ceremonial paint, blue in color.

    The next trial paired the cubs into teams of two. Their task was to go into the wilds and hunt as a pack, to bring down the largest prey they could find. Their success would be determined on whether or not they came back with their prize and their lives. Vladimir looked at the cub he had been paired with. A young woman by the name of Gia like the Titan of the Earth she was large and well built, she was pretty if not beautiful, a turned Lycanthrope if memory served Vladimir right. She eyed him with appreciation like he was a piece of meat on the butchers block for sale. He knew she fancied him, most of the young women of the pack fancied him.

But only because they could not have him, as everyone in the pack figured him to be a bad apple, a menace, dangerous. As much as he desired to prove the pack wrong about him however it would not stop Vladimir from taking advantage of the situation to place himself higher in the ranks of the competing cubs, nothing was going to stop him from becoming a man by the packs eyes and proving to the entire pack that he was a man to be respected, even feared.
"Let me lead the hunt Gia, I know the woods well and we will find good prey this night." Vladimir stated slowly, talking to Gia as he would a fond friend, offering her his hand a friendly smile on his face. His every move was a step to bring her to the conclusion that he was her friend and not simply using her to his benefit.

Gia took his hand eagerly and shook, more than willing to let him lead the hunt. Vladimir shifted his form and took the lead as Gia followed him. He led her through the forest to an area that he knew well enough to avoid when he was alone and on other business. They were miles away from the village now. There was no one out here to help them, Vladimir shifted into his half form motioning for Gia to do the same as he approached a large cave. His sensitive eyes could make out the form of his prey and he suppressed an instinctual growl.

    The forest rang with an angry roar as the beast charged out of the cave at them; Vladimir braced himself to receive the charge and locked his arms around the beast's neck keeping the dangerous fangs away from his face and neck as his own teeth dug into flesh while Gia attacked the beast's rear, latching onto the beast's leg. The beast in question was a great black bear of giant size and unusual strength; Vladimir wrestled with it for several long moments, each trying to gain the upper hand over the other.

    Vladimir was grateful for Gia's presence as she kept the bear distracted enough that the beast could not rear up and grab a hold of Vladimir to squeeze him. He would have been in a tight spot then. Rolling his shoulders Vladimir rotated the bears head up at an odd angle and drove his arms down with all his strength, snapping the beasts' neck, the bear fell lifeless at Vladimir's feet and he grabbed the corpse and heaved lifting it into the air. Gia also grabbed hold and helped carry the burden. The going was slow as they made their way back to the village. When they returned they returned last, but with the largest kill, the other cubs had stuck to killing smaller game and had not risked going after such large and dangerous prey. Vladimir had again shocked the Task Masters when Gia recounted their hunt to them, Vladimir bore the majority of the injuries from the bear as he had been in reach of the things claws. Though he had not felt anything initially, but eventually he had felt the bitter sting as he had carried most of the bear's weight back to the village.

    The Task masters were forced to paint both Gia and Vladimir with the purple ceremonial paint but in the pattern of the highest honor, the mark of the wolf, with the face of the wolf on their chest and two marks descending like fangs down their backs. Next was the Trial of Valor, where the cubs would be pitted against each other to fight for the Honor and Glory of the pack, for the right to become a man in the eyes of the pack. They were not allowed to shift their forms or have any other weapons in the circle than their bodies. But Vladimir had learned in the last six years from his father that sometimes your body was the only weapon you needed in any fight. His father had trained him to use his fists and body as a weapon more efficiently in battle and in hunting and naturally Vladimir was a quick learner and hungry for knowledge. Now he was eager to prove his skills in battle.

    Vladimir stood inside the circle waiting for his opponent, the cub who had the second highest ranking. He quite naturally had the first, a ranking the Task Masters had begrudgingly bestowed. Vladimir may not have been accepted or even welcome, but the Task Masters were fair at least to participating males, female cubs were not generally welcome in this male dominated society, even in his mother's pack. A large part of that had to do with the love and respect they held for Vladimir's mother, Lady Shadow, the

Queen of the Northern Packs. His opponent stepped into the circle and Vladimir looked him over, he recognized the youth as one of the many young cubs that had tormented him throughout his child hood.

The youths name was Braxen, the son of his mother's Beta, Stephan and he was a brazen youth charging straight in with a roar that would have intimidated any lesser opponent when the Task Masters started the fight. Vladimir took the first blow on his chest. It stung a little but was no worse than getting flicked by a child, in Vladimir's eyes he had suffered much worse. By setting himself purposefully to take the hit and lock with his opponent as he had with the bear he was setting his opponent up for failure. This time his strong arms wrapped around those of his opponent driving them down and wide before pushing the youth away. It was his turn to issue forth a challenge; Vladimir summoned all the strength of his lungs as he bellowed his challenge. His voice ringing fourth in a deep thundering roar that had most of the crowd covering their ears.

The youth stumbled and fell back against the ring of spectators. They pushed him back into the ring and towards Vladimir their blood lust was up and they wanted to see the best of the pack fight it out for superiority.

The youth had fear in his eyes now, Vladimir's roar had shaken him, but Vladimir was guessing that it was another reason that was making the youth flee him. Vladimir was by no means a small man at six feet tall and packed with muscle, he had the build of an Ancient warrior and he had a reputation amongst the pack as a dangerous and deadly fighter. A reputation he had earned after killing not just the Barrett child but after killing nine more opponents in the last six years, two of which were other cubs that had tried to take him out while he was sleeping, the other seven were members of another pack that had attacked in the night. Vladimir had stayed when his mother ordered the cubs to flee and he had attacked the back of the enemy packs ranks. Killing not only the rival packs Beta, but the Alpha as well, taking five other full grown

Lycanthropes down before he himself was overwhelmed and brought down. And right now he had murder in his eyes, the youth tried to flee the circle, perhaps fearing for his life and rightly so.

Vladimir growled as the youth was pushed back into the circle. He stood straight and said softly but loud enough for the entire pack to hear.
"If he wants to run, let him run, he only dishonors himself; this is a Trial of Valor, of Bravery and Courage." He spread his arms wide expanding his chest as he inhaled proclaiming loudly. "Regardless the reputation of your opponent, regardless the size or the skill of the man before you, you are expected to show no fear and charge him down that is the Valor you are expected to show." Vladimir bared his fangs so they gleamed in the moon light.
"I cannot pass this trial without a challenger, is there any one of you willing to take me on? I will take any number of you on." Vladimir declared spinning in a circle, "Cub or man come face me and test your mettle." He smiled as six of the

strongest members of the pack stepped into the ring.

Vladimir stood over the broken forms of his opponents and roared, he was covered in bruises and gashes but he was the one standing and the six men were not. He glanced up at his mother and saw his father standing there. Both of them were beaming at him while the rest of the onlookers looked at him in stunned silence. The Task Masters came into the ring after they regained their senses and painted him with the ceremonial black paint declaring him an adult by pack law, he did not just earn that black body paint but the white death mask that came with the killing at least one of his opponents.

Vladimir turned around and walked out of the ring. Making his way his parents, Vladimir bowed his head to his father and mother before walking away and heading to the cabin that he and his mother shared. He was not one for festivals or celebrations not that he was usually included anyways, it was better not to participate then force your presence on people who wanted nothing to do with you.

Volume One

Chapter Four

Looking around at the luxurious suite that had been provided for him, Vladimir growled and looked around for his bags. He did not know what half the things in this room were let alone what they were used for. It took him awhile to find all of his things in the room, then he explored the suite, finding the facilities and a study attached to his main room. Vladimir searched the study and found a thick, leather bound book, it was a heavy tome. But when he opened it the pages were blank save one. The first page detailed a family tree, near the bottom Vladimir saw his parents' names, and underneath them, his own.

He assumed that because he was a man by pack law now, and had proven he could take care of himself well enough that his father would finally claim him as his own. It was a dangerous ploy; the Emperor would not suffer a half breed to live for very long. Not unless Vladimir proved himself invaluable, a nearly insurmountable task in and of itself. Sighing Vladimir closed the

Volume One

book and a voice spoke from behind him. Vladimir tensed up preparing for an attack.

"It is a Compendium Immortalis; you will record your history in it." Vladimir relaxed recognizing the voice as belonging to his father. He turned to view his father, and watched as the man walked further into the room. "Your grandfather will not like that I have claimed you, so you will have to work hard to prove you are an asset to the Empire." His father continued, the man went to the desk and uncapped a bottle of ink and dipped a quill into it. He turned to Vladimir and smiled, baring his fangs in the light of the sun that came through the window, as he held the quill out to Vladimir. When Vladimir took it his father's smile brightened.

"That is why, in two weeks' time I will send you to the Academy where you will be given a formal Immortal education." His father said lightly before moving away back to the door, he touched Vladimir's shoulder and said. "You will spend the next twenty four years there learning and serving the Empire. Prove to the world that you deserve to live." Vladimir growled as his father left him alone in his room.

He looked at the book on his desk and sat down. Taking the quill he brought the nib to the page making the first strokes of many. Detailing all of his life that he could remember until that moment, his handwriting was small and cramped but quick and sure. Making him fill the first ten pages quickly, he did not leave out details or his thoughts and he wrote in the Ancient language of the Immortals, this way if another Immortal was to read it the task would be easier. His mother had explained the importance of a Compendium Immortalis though it was not a tradition that Lycanthropes followed, they passed their stories and histories on as oral histories.

Vladimir did not try to get settled into his new environment over the next two weeks, he was not going to be here long. He did however find his father's forge and workshop while his father was working in it the day before his departure for the Academy. Watching from the doorway as his father forged a piece of metal into

Volume One

a fine blade, Vladimir was mesmerized. This was something that he wanted to learn as he watched the masterful flow of muscle as his father guided the hammer to shape the blade that he was working. Vladimir did not think he had seen anything so violently peaceful.

Feeling Vladimir's eyes upon him, his father stopped and looked at the piece before turning his head and looking at Vladimir and asking roughly.

"Did I catch your interest?" Vladimir nodded quietly, lost for words and came closer to the blade his father was annealing. "Then when you graduate from the Academy I will begin teaching you the arts of making, everything I know I will teach you." Vladimir nodded and went to a set of carving tools hanging on the wall.

Since he knew his father was not much of a warrior, he had always wondered how he'd won his mothers heart. Vladimir tapped a chisel and turned to face his father.

"Is this how you won mother's heart?" he asked softly, his father chuckled and Vladimir watched his father shrug.

"Your mother is not one for fine gifts and luxury, though she is the queen of the pack." His father said lightly. "I wooed your mother carefully and at great peril to myself, I was under the impression that she hated me the whole time and that I was going to annoy her so much she was going to rip my throat out." Vladimir grinned that certainly sounded like his mother. "What was it that finally won mother over?" Vladimir asked, his father cocked his head to the side and went to a chest. He pulled out a worn leather book and placed it on his anvil next to the cooling sword.

"I gave her this, my Compendium Immortalis and a sword." His father said as he tapped the book with his finger. "And I told her if she did not find me suitable that she should take the sword and kill me because I would not be able to live without her." Vladimir came closer and looked at the worn book, noting that it was roughly the same size as his own, but he doubted there was a single page left blank there were probably several other volumes other than this one. He looked back at his father and asked.

"What was mother's response to you?" his father chuckled and pulled a small ball of metal out of the chest.

"She read my Compendium and returned the sword to me in a knot of steel telling me that if I ever betrayed her she would not hesitate to rip my throat out with her teeth." He said taking the book off the anvil and returning it and the small ball of metal to the chest.

His father was silent for a long while before he began to speak again.

"Let me tell you the best way to win any Lady is to literally give them a piece of yourself, there is nothing more personal than your life's story, and you would do well to remember that." Vladimir nodded and turned his attention back to the sword on the anvil, the blade was half as long as Vladimir himself and the blade was broad. Going from maybe a hands breadth at the base before narrowing gradually along the length of the blade until it reached the end it was a bit of an older fashioned sword. Made for hacking through armor, sinew, and bone. It was an elegant weapon of war.

His father pulled the blade off the anvil and moved over to the workbench on the other side of the workshop and Vladimir's attention was caught by a sword already in its sheath. The crosspiece was a simple solid piece of highly polished silver, and the hilt was wrapped with thick polished silver wire, and the pommel was capped with a snarling silver wolfs head.

His father smiled at him and presented him with the sheathed sword as the sun was going down.
"A going away present for you, you will need it where you will be going." He said slowly as Vladimir took the blade feeling the weight of the sword in his hand, he drew it easily out of its sheath and taking a few steps out of the work shop he swung it through the air loving the balance that the sword had, he inspected the pattern of running wolves that weaved down the blade with affection. This was a wondrous tool for killing mortals and Immortals, made of the purest Immortal steel. This weapon would carry

Vladimir to great heights; Vladimir could feel it in his bones and reverberating in his hand as he swung the sword. This sword was perfect, for him.

His father returned to the work bench and held out a belt and belt buckle.

 "Put it on; let us see how it looks on you." He said as he came outside to join Vladimir. Vladimir took the belt and belt buckle and noticed that the belt buckle was shaped like the head of a wolf. He slipped the belt around his waist and fastened the sword to it and secured the belt, letting it settle around his hips. Vladimir rested his hand on the pommel of the sword, he had used weapons in battle before, and his mother had made sure he had learned how to use weapons in general.

So he was not uncomfortable wearing the sword, but he would have been more comfortable without it, using his claws and fangs would have been preferable. His father caught his look and said softly.
"You can use any weapon you feel comfortable with, whether they be your claws or the sword

but you will need all the help you can get." His father sighed and walked away leaving Vladimir to think on what he said.

    The following morning dawned bright and found Vladimir dressed in a simple linen tunic and leather breaches and calf high boots his ebony hair bound back by a silver circlet. The boots fit him well and were molded to his feet. His father had sent him to a skilled cobbler for them. It was like he was not wearing anything at all which is what he was used to. The sword his father had made him hung comfortably at his waist, and a pouch with money hung on his belt near the sword, in his hands was a roll of parchment with his name, his parents' names, their house names and sealed with the Royal seal, proof of his pedigree.

    He may be a half breed, but he was a half breed of two pure blooded Immortals and not just any pure blooded Immortals but two Immortals from the two purest lines of the Immortal peoples. His father was from an original Ancient line of Immortals, the Royals and his mother was from the oldest, purest line of Lycanthropes in existence. The Academy only accepted Nobles, thus the papers proving his pedigree. Vladimir waited in the front hall of his father's castle; he was waiting for the carriage that would take him to the Academy. His father was not waiting with him, his father had greeted him at breakfast but they had no more contact than that.

When the carriage arrived and his luggage was loaded onto it, Vladimir climbed in without a second thought, without even looking back at the castle and wondering when he would return. He knew that if he was to return, he would return a changed man. As his father put it, the Academy had a way of changing people either for the better or for the worst. Vladimir was going to have to find a way to survive the Academy and its challenges on his own. The carriage bounced along the road jostling Vladimir and making it almost impossible for him to get comfortable.

He would have felt safer running outside the contraption, and travel probably would have been much faster. The driver was singing as he drove and the mere sound of it was driving

Vladimir insane. The day passed slowly as Vladimir watched the land pass him by, they were going at a fair pace he could hear the horses' even breathing and the straining of the harnesses as the six great beasts pulled the laden carriage down the road. He sighed and settled against the padding of the seat and resigned himself to a long ride.

It took four weeks to reach the hidden Immortal metropolis in the heart of a wide cold mountain range. Vladimir looked around him at the wide avenues and broad stone buildings in awe, the carriage drove right through the Immortal capital city Coelum and up into the mountains to a complex of tall simple buildings behind a high wall. The carriage pulled up to a set of heavy iron gates, standing before these gates was a single diminutive man wearing a breast plate over his chest, greaves on his legs, plated boots on his feet and bracers on his forearms. His head was capped with a decorated open faced helm. At his side was a stout broad bladed sword with a highly decorated hilt in a leather sheath on a heavy belt.

Once the carriage stopped completely Vladimir stepped out and walked to the man, he towered over the man by over three feet. The man's pale blue eyes looked him over and the man held his hand out wordlessly for his papers and Vladimir handed them over. The man read the papers over and his eyes popped open in surprise at what he had read but he quickly recovered.

"Young Prince, I am Commander Chase and *I* run this institution." The man said with a bow, Vladimir looked him over again and nodded to himself. The man certainly had an air of authority to him and Vladimir thought he would not be a man to cross despite his size. "I see that your paperwork is in order please follow me, once you enter these doors Young Prince, your title will mean nothing, and until you prove you are something then you are nothing." Vladimir withheld a growl and bowed his head sharply grabbing his few bags from the carriage he followed Commander Chase through the gates that had cracked open slightly to admit them.

Commander Chase showed him to the barracks and to his bunk; Vladimir was the object of much attention as Commander Chase was talking loudly and unabashedly with Vladimir about his needs.

"Your father is Royal, so I assume you will need to feed, and your mother is the Lady of the forest so I assume you can shift your shape." He said loudly as he came to a stop before Vladimir's bunk. "You will be trained like any other cadet in this Academy; you will be treated like any other cadet in this Academy at least by the instructors of this Academy, if you need to feed go to the feeding houses for what you need at the appropriate times of course." The Commander looked at the rest of the barracks and proclaimed to the whole hall.

"Remember on your lives you dogs that he may be your fellow cadet but he is also a member of the Royal Family." Commander Chase declared hand on the hilt of his sword. "Regardless of what you feel about his breeding remember that fact, remember what punishment awaits you when he or his father is Emperor because I assure you neither of them will forget." With that Commander Chase left the hall and left it abuzz with murmurings.

Vladimir looked around the room at the Immortals around him; the amount of Nobles in the room astounded him there were maybe fifty young Immortals in the hall, quite a number of younglings for the not so prolific Immortal race. He could see the flash of green in a few eyes that indicated a few of them were of lycanthropic descent. But they were few compared to the amount of Vampires in the room. Not one tried to approach him, though they all inhaled deeply of his scent and eyed him warily. Vladimir smiled to himself, and shook his head. It seemed he simply went from one hostile situation to another.

His mother's pack had never accepted him, had barely even tolerated him. And in the two weeks he was with his father he had received somewhat better treatment by his father's staff, but none of them actually liked him or considered him their equal. Even to the servants he was less than human, he was just royal and they had to treat him with a modicum of status. Here it was back to when he was just a cub, but now they were wary of him. They did not know what he could do; they did not know what he was capable of and just how good his standing was with his family. One wrong step could end their lives or their political careers.

When the lights went out in the hall Vladimir was writing in his Compendium, he wrote by moonlight for a bit longer before putting the book in the chest at the foot of his cot. He pulled the blankets up around his neck and laid his sword next to him on the cot. Vladimir lay awake for a long time listening to the whispers that circulated around the hall. The main topic of discussion was him, and how long he was going to last, the whispers died down when a hoarse whisper said softly. "...He's already a killer, I watched him shred seven full grown Immortals and one of them was an Alpha of another pack while he was still just a cub, and I do not need to explain that Alphas are the most powerful members of the pack." The voice said softly there was a long pause before it continued. "He is a daemon of the night, a half bred monstrosity, he shouldn't even exist..." Vladimir smirked to himself as he recognized the voice to belong to Braxen, the youth that had fled from him in the trial of cubs. It fit since he was the son of his mother's Beta, a foul tempered intolerant man that despised him to no end, he was a minor noble. But he was a coward, and a shameful one at that, so Stephan had probably sent him here to buck up. Vladimir shifted in his cot and spoke softly and menacingly.

"That's right I am a Daemon, I am a half breed monstrosity just as you say." Vladimir held his sword tight as his eyes gleamed in the moonlight coming in through the windows. "You say I should never have existed, but here I am and I hold a position in life higher than any of you could ever dream because I am a Prince of the Immortal Empire." Silence resounded and Vladimir settled down into his thin pillow.

The silence reigned for moments longer as the others in the room contemplated what he said and their positions in life compared to his.

Vladimir knew very well that he held a high position, but he also knew his grandfather, the Emperor's views on half breeds. His high position was lofty and would have some pull if he could put a reputation behind himself instead of relying on his fathers and his mothers. He already had the beginnings of a reputation thanks to Braxen, the reputation of a demon of the night. Now he just had to make it work for him. He needed to make an image for himself, build his reputation as an honorable but ruthless man. For that he needed to build on what Braxen had given him and prove himself useful to the Empire. That was also the only way he was going to survive this place.

    Vladimir was the first of the cadets up in the morning, dressed in his Academy uniform with his sword belted at his waist. The windows were still dark, but Vladimir was wide awake, he did not wait for the sound of the summoning horn to summon him and the rest of the cadets to assemble, his father had given him the rundown on how the Academy operated. Slowly the other cadets woke and began getting ready for the day, with varying degrees of reluctance. Vladimir returned his attention to his cot making double sure that it was made neatly. The sky had barely begun to lighten when the horns sounded for them to assemble. Vladimir led the rest of the cadets out into the main yard of the Academy. Commander Chase stood on a dais next to a tall whip of a man holding the Royal Banner. He looked at the assembled cadets and spoke, his voice carrying through the entire courtyard.

"As those of you Vampires can probably tell I am indeed a Lycanthrope." He said laying a hand on his sword hilt as he spoke. "Therefore it is without a doubt that you think that I am beneath you, make no mistake younglings *I am* the *master* here I do not serve you, regardless of your family rank or position as long as you are here in this Academy *you* serve me." Vladimir listened to the cadets around him, the Lycanthropes accepted their positions readily they could sense the fact that the Commander was without a doubt an Alpha, a powerful one, but the Vampires they broke rank with outbursts of outrage.

"We serve you! You should be executed for even saying such things!" one of the cadets snarled falling into a crouch; Commander Chase cocked his head to the side and bared his fangs.

"Is that a challenge boy?" he growled as he straightened, his posture was loose and relaxed the pose of an experienced warrior.

Vladimir kept his eyes on the Commander as the challenging youth took a step towards the dais. No one tried to stop him; in fact there were several encouraging remarks from the Vampires in the ranks. The Vampire drew his sword and leveled it at the Commander. Laughter resounded from the ranks of Vampires, catcalls, and mocking jeers encouraging the youth to speak.

"Dogs that do not understand their place in the world should be put down." The youth snarled as he approached, he had the stalk of a confident predator, Vladimir knew that confidence was going to get the youth killed. He could see it in the Commander's eyes; the

Commander was going to make an example of this young Vampire. The Commander looked at the Vampire calmly and asked.

"And are you going to put me down youngling?" the young Vampire reached the dais and started up the steps; Vladimir put his hand on the hilt of his sword. When the youth fell, one of two things was going to happen either the rest of the Vampires in the group would shut up and fall in line, or all hell would break loose and there would be more bloodshed. It was then that Vladimir noticed the whip on the Commander's belt. It was obvious that the Commander had dealt with these situations before. He took his hand off the hilt of his sword and relaxed; he would wait and see what the Commander was going to do with this group of rambunctious younglings.

    The Vampire youth reached the top of the dais and swung his sword, thinking the Commander would do nothing to defend himself. After all the youth was a Vampire and had probably been raised to believe that the Lycanthropes were less than them, no better than human. Vladimir watched as the youth's head came free of his shoulders with a spray of blood that splattered the Commanders breast plate and the steps, before the head fell and rolled back down the steps to the first line of cadets.

The Commander snapped the whip off his belt as the others went to step forward and took the next Vampire that started up the dais stairs off their feet. Cautiously the rest held back, though their fangs were bared and their eyes shone with livid fury. Commander Chase snapped the whip through the air and against the ground with a crack.
"That is ENOUGH!" he bellowed stunning them all into silence. Having now garnered their attention he continued in a slow hiss. "Each and every one of you is here to complete twenty four years of the most brutal military training in this Empire; many of you will not survive the first year, you will either die or quit." The Commander held his arms out to give them a clear view of his bloodied breastplate.

The small man pointed at the cadets with his bloodied sword and continued speaking softly.

"Forget *all* preconceived notions of superiority that your parents have given you for here you are *all* equal, here you will *all* rise and fall by your *own* will, by your *own* power." Commander Chase growled at them. "Superiority over all others comes from excellence of self, from the utter commitment to survive by *any* means, the commitment to rise *above* your fellows and *lead* them." The Commander lowered his sword and wiped the blade on the dead cadet's uniform before sheathing it.

Coiling his whip again in his hand, he came down the steps of the dais, followed by the banner bearing Immortal. Many of the cadets were several feet taller than him as he approached. He spoke loudly and with authority barking his words to them now.

"Every morning before the fifth sounding of the summoning horn you mongrels will be assembled here in the courtyard swiftly, orderly, and silently for the sound off." He said as he eyed them dangerously, Vladimir met his eyes and knew this man would not hesitate to whip him within an inch of his life if he made a single mistake, if he broke a single one of this man's unbending rules. "Before you even report to the feeding hall, you all will complete a one hundred mile hike through the surrounding mountains, in full gear, carrying that." The Commander pointed to a five foot high block of stone that was twenty five feet long with twenty five steel rods placed evenly on the side that Vladimir could see of the block he assumed that the rods continued onto the other side. Commander Chase rolled his head cracking his neck loudly before barking.

"What are you all standing around for? Go grab your armor and gear and get going." The whip cracked sending those nearest to him running. Vladimir followed to the armory and outfitted himself in the full armor of a Royal Knight, which was what he would become if he survived the Academy and the service to the Empire. Next was the heavy framed backpack filled near to bursting with the essentials, and a bedroll rolled and strapped to the bottom. Vladimir pulled on his equipment silently and took up his position by the block of stone.

The cadets quickly learned that in order to lift the stone and carry it over the rough terrain of the mountains they had to work together. Though this took many brawls to establish a marching order and an order of leadership, of which Vladimir took control of very quickly. The hike was going badly, the sun was raising high in the sky and tempers were rising. Vladimir worked quickly to keep the peace setting himself up as a dominating factor of the group. Taking charge and putting things in order, he could sense the resentment of everyone in the group but no one else was up to the task.

No one else was willing to step up and claim the responsibility for the entire group of cadets. Vladimir led them through the day and back to the Academy before the sun set. He also led them into the feeding hall, though he separated himself from them and headed to a private room. When the cadets emerged for the final sound off, Commander Chase was waiting for them.

"Listen well mongrels, the armor you are in is the armor you will graduate in, take good care of it, it may mean your life if you do not." he said softly he looked at Vladimir and smirked. "Then again it may mean your life if you do not listen to your Commander, well done Vladimir that is the kind of attitude that will earn you renown." Vladimir bowed his head in respect.

"Thank you Commander." He muttered. The Commander nodded and put his fist on his chest a gesture of respect.

"But remember leaders are often the object of would be assassins." Commander Chase said with a smug smirk. "Lights out in twenty, get some rest you will need it." the Commander said as he turned to leave. Vladimir led the rest of the cadets back to the barracks, where he opened his Compendium and began writing the days experiences down.

Chapter Five

The first ten years of the Academy passed for Vladimir in almost the blink of an eye; he grew into his leadership role and excelled in it, gaining rank and renown almost immediately. He built around himself a flawless reputation, the reputation of a resourceful, smart, capable, and ruthless man. Vladimir learned the politics game quickly and played it quite willingly, doing everything in his power he could to gain the upper hand over his fellow cadets and survive. In this time under the grueling physical and mental conditions of the Academy, Vladimir mastered both his mind and body; he needed both to be on constant alert as the Commander was right. His leadership position, obvious natural skill and authority often made him the target for assassination attempts and assault.

He was nearly always on the constant edge of paranoia; his sleep was light and fitful at best. His food sources had been poisoned on more than one occasion, but his sense of smell and taste saved him. Most poisons give of a subtle scent or taste, no matter what it was concealed in, whether it be the blood stream of a donor or in a plate of food. Others though, gave no scent at all, or diminished the scents of whatever it was that it was in. A sure sign that something was amiss was that subtle odor or lack thereof, the next was taste. Vladimir hardly minded the lack of sleep, or the fact that it pushed him to the limits of his endurance and beyond. He remained cool and collected hard as it was at times, gathering about himself his reputation, the pivotal point on which his survival rested. If he was to prove to his grandfather that he was an asset, that he deserved to live, then he would need to increase his reputation and far more than that to survive.

    In those ten years that Vladimir rose through the Academy ranks, earning his reputation and making his mark, the number of cadets around him dwindled. By the end of the first ten years only ten of the other cadets remained besides Vladimir, two Lycanthropes and eight Vampires. The others had either died or quit. Nearly twenty of the cadets that had died had met their untimely demises at Vladimir's hands either in struggles over power or in pathetic assassination attempts. The most notable of them all was the coward Braxen's death. The sniveling fool had tried to cut Vladimir's throat in his sleep. Vladimir had not been pleased, nor had he stayed his hand and eased Braxen's death; no that was something Vladimir reserved only for the opponents that he respected to some degree, he made Braxen suffer before the end and he made sure that every single person in the Academy knew what he had done.

It was with Braxen's death that the whispers of the Academies fearsome demon reached out into the world, carrying his name into the metropolis of the Immortals along with his reputation and the title he had begun to be known by in those ten years. Prince Vladimir, the Daemon Wolf. He was feared and respected by the remaining cadets and the instructors of the Academy. The only person who treated him with any degree of normalcy was Commander Chase, who was not intimidated by Vladimir in the slightest, but did respect the youth's prowess and natural ability to lead.

    The next stage of the cadet's journey into Knighthood was their fourteen years of service to the Empire as elite soldiers. Vladimir donned his armor and gear before leading the remainder of his platoon out to the courtyard to meet their new Commanding officer. The person that would lead them into battle and to glory for the Empire, the person whose orders they would have to follow or die. Lining his fellow cadets up Vladimir stood before them and inspected them thoroughly before stepping aside and allowing Commander Chase to take it from there. Commander Chase looked them over and nodded to himself. There was a clattering of wheels and a carriage was driven into the courtyard. Vladimir having excelled not only in the physical aspects of the Academy but the institutional as well recognized the Royal Seal on the carriage and reacted accordingly as it pulled to a stop before the dais.

    Drawing his sword and saluting as two figures stepped out of the carriage. One he

instantly recognized as his father, the other was a man similar in build and physical appearance to his father, with the exception of his eyes. This man's eyes were gold in color and as piercing as any knife. The rest of the cadets followed his example as they saw who it was, their delayed reaction causing Vladimir to scowl. It was obvious who this unknown man was, Vladimir had seen portraits of him throughout the Academy and he was shocked. He hadn't expected his grandfather to show up. Commander Chase bowed his head and crossed one hand over his breast plate and took a step down on the dais.
"Lord Emperor and Crown Prince Vladimir, what gives us the fine pleasure of your visit this fine day?" Commander Chase asked lightly as he stared at his feet.

    The gold eyed man did not speak to the Commander his eyes were locked on Vladimir in a look of utter disgust, the same look that Vladimir had lived with all his life with his mother's pack. Like his grandfather was viewing something singularly unpleasant and stomach turning, like a rotting corpse or some other foul thing. Noting the look that his father was giving his son Vladimir's father spoke instead, trying to get the necessities out of the way as quickly as possible before his father did something drastic. "We have come to inspect the cadets before they ascend to their next step in their long journey." He said lightly with a tense smile his eyes slipping to Vladimir who was staring fixedly ahead like he did not see either his grandfather or his father. He was fully aware of how his grandfather was viewing him and knew that his grandfather without a doubt knew who and what he was.

    Vladimir gave the order to drop the salute and stood at attention as his father and Commander Chase discussed things in low tones on the dais. This was interrupted by a smooth melodic voice that spoke softly and sinisterly. The words that were uttered made Vladimir's heart sink in his chest, he knew his father would be unable to do anything to circumvent this without putting his own life at risk. Neither of them could risk that, if both of them died Vladimir's mother would be heartbroken, if the shock did not kill her first. From the look Vladimir caught on his father's face out of the corner of his eye Vladimir knew that his father was feeling the same thing.

"I want to see each of the cadets compete against each other in a free for all matches to the death." The voice said silkily before continuing softly, just loud enough for the whole courtyard to hear. "The survivor will become a Royal Knight immediately." Vladimir knew instinctively that this was a ploy to get the other cadets to kill him; the worst part was that it was going to work. But he did not earn the name Daemon Wolf for nothing. He was not the highest ranking officer in the cadet ranks for nothing. He was not one of the most accomplished swordsmen in the Academy for no reason. Vladimir had devoted every free waking hour to mastering every weapon he had available to him, his entire body was a weapon and his sword was an extension of himself.

He felt confident that even if all ten of the remaining cadets came at him at once he would be fine, though very hard pressed. Commander Chase snapped his head into a bow and drew his sword and flicked the whip off his belt. His face was cold as stone, but he was sweating profusely and his eyes betrayed his worry as his eyes met with Vladimir's as if to speak an apology.

"You heard the Emperor you maggots, give him a fight worth the legends." Commander Chase snarled snapping his whip at them and setting them into action. Vladimir put his hand on his sword hilt as the other cadets started to surround him, needling him with their swords. He snarled warningly as his shift began, giving him an advantage and drew the blade as the crowd pressed in.

Vladimir wielded his blade, claws, and fangs artfully and soon the paved courtyard was slick with blood. Four of the ten were already dead, their torn bodies lying at his feet. But Vladimir was wounded as well his blood ran freely from a dozen deep wounds about his chest and arms his armor was rent and dented in several places. Still he was a tireless machine using claws, fangs, and steel to rend the life from his opponents in a graceful dance that left onlookers stunned with the display. Even his grandfather was silent to watch the ongoing battle though his face was twisted into a visage of disdain and disgust. Like he could not believe that the half breed was winning against multiple pureblood opponents and doing so with more skill and grace than some of his finest Knights. Vladimir's father watched the spectacle with anxious and awed eyes as his son darted through the courtyard dodging blow after blow and returning them with equal ferocity.

    As the battle neared its bloody end the Emperor's golden eyes were unemotional and watched with a coldness that had even the Commander nervous. As the last of the cadets fell at Vladimir's feet as he retreated up the dais. He turned to face his grandfather and father and fell to one knee; blood coated his armor and matted his hair dripping down his face and hands, Vladimir having had shifted back to his human form. Vladimir raised his head to meet his grandfather's eyes and offered the man his sword hilt first. The man took it and raised it above his head like he was going to strike Vladimir down, but brought it to rest gently on Vladimir's shoulder, tapping each shoulder gently.

    The metal of the blade clinking against the metal of Vladimir's armor Vladimir's grandfather lowered the sword to Vladimir's throat and growled.
"Rise Prince Vladimir son of my son and know that if you should stray but an inch I will not hesitate to kill you." Vladimir rose hardly feeling the point of his sword as it dug into his throat. He understood that his grandfather would not hesitate to kill him regardless. The man would probably send assassins after him from now on. "You are a Knight of the Royal Guard, you will return home with your father for a period of ten years to learn what that means after that you will be assigned to a post." With that the Emperor dropped the sword at Vladimir's feet and descended the dais climbing into his carriage with the ease and grace of a lion. Vladimir reached down to retrieve his sword,

feeling drained and elated at the same time. His father caught him as he slumped into unconsciousness taken by his wounds.

They stayed in Coelum for a period of two weeks waiting for Vladimir to recover enough to travel. His father went over many things with him, but only touched the most basic of the basics of the Code of Conduct carried by a Knight of the Royal Guard. The Royal Guard was a bastion of honor, of morality. They held to strict codes of behavior that was law unto all Knights that belonged to the order. The first thing Vladimir's father instilled into him was that the overriding, most unbending law of the Royal Guard was that you obeyed all orders to the letter no matter what the order was. You carried out your orders without question, no matter what they were.

When Vladimir asked his father why he was so adamant about this his father's only response was to shake his head and say.
"If you want to survive in the world you are about to enter, do as I say and remember my words well because they will keep you alive."

Vladimir was not satisfied with his father's answer and growled back.

"And what if it calls into question my honor? Or the honor of every Knight that I am with?" Vladimir asked softly as his father turned to leave the room, his father sighed and came back to his bedside.

"When you find yourself questioning your honor, and the honor of your companions." He said slowly putting his hand on Vladimir's Compendium. "Remember there is honor and dignity in choosing to live so that one day when you have the power you can be the guiding hand behind the Knight's Morality even if that means following your orders or orders that goes against your morals." He turned again and left without saying another word to Vladimir. His message had been cryptic and kept Vladimir up for hours after he was supposed to have gone to bed.

When they returned to the castle the lessons began in earnest. Vladimir absorbed the knowledge his father gave him like a sponge and even expanded upon it as he spent most of his free time in the library when he could be spared from the forge or his father's study. He filled nearly five thick leather tomes with all the information that he learned on his own. While he was in the library he read anything and everything he could dig up about the Royal Guard and his grandfather. If anything happened he wanted to be prepared for it. The Royal Guard had its beginnings with the first Emperor an Ancient whose name could be roughly translated to Arthur the son of the Wild, King of the North. As the Ancients were known before the Empire, before Vladimir's family had all but wiped them out in a long and bloody war that created the Vampires and Lycanthropes.

The Royal Guard was made up of the elite of the two Immortal races that had been created; they were designed to police the new Empire, to keep the peace. They were the long reaching arm of the Emperor they were his judge, his jury, and the swift falling axe of his anger. Because the methods of training these new soldiers were so brutal not many survived, but those that did soon became the jewels of the crown. Not many were needed so only the Nobles of the two races were chosen to become members of the Royal Guard thus the need for a pedigree. The Knights of the Royal Guard were a devastating force, pure destruction and devastation by all accounts.

    As Vladimir read he came to feel slightly uneasy about his new title, Honor and morality could mean many things depending on who you asked and clearly his orders would be coming from his grandfather. Who did not strike him as a man who would spare a single child if one villager betrayed him. Vladimir calmed himself in the forge working on perfecting that craft as his father's lessons rang in his head. As the metal was shaped beneath his hands into beautiful pieces of art Vladimir reflected on his father's lessons and memorized them.

    In those ten years with his father, Vladimir spent every waking hour he could spare away from his lessons or his studying in the forge, perfecting that craft as much as time would allow him. He knew though he would have many more years of learning ahead of him before he could even begin to produce the level of work his father could. Within a year Vladimir had learned all his father had to teach him everything about the Knights of the Royal Guard; the rest was applying it in the real world. There were many parties held in Vladimir's honor. Now that his father had claimed him as his own and he was recognized as a Prince of the Royal family, he had to be brought before the court Nobles and presented as such.

    Many of the court Nobles were curious about him but wary of him at the same time. They had heard of him, of the Daemon Wolf of the Academy. For Vladimir the parties were singularly uncomfortable to attend. Most of the young Court Nobles that attended the parties had a pretty young thing on their arm to dance with. As host and Prince he reserved the right to dance with every Lady in the room and any man he took fancy to, in fact it was something that his father insisted on. But this was not the simplistic dancing of his mother's pack. This was the sophisticated dancing of the Ancients and Vampires. There were several Lycanthrope Nobles present but they tended to stay off the dance floor and to the side where they were more comfortable.

There was one young noble woman who was unafraid of Vladimir; she was quite young by her scent. Her sire's blood still coursed strong in her veins stinging Vladimir's nose as she approached. She was a tall, well-endowed woman, with a generous bust, a slim waist and wide hips, accented perfectly by her gown. Her chestnut hair hung in ringlets down her back, framing her heart shaped face. Vladimir could not deny that she was a beautiful woman; she had his attention as she sauntered up to him waving a delicate fan. She held out a delicate hand for him and Vladimir kissed the back of it gently as she introduced herself.

"Lady Olivia, eldest daughter of Lord Artair." She said in a sultry voice that gave him chills. Vladimir bowed his head releasing her hand and putting his arm over his breast to introduce himself.

"It is a pleasure to meet you Lady Olivia; I am Prince Vladimir, son of Crown Prince Vladimir and Lady Shadow of the forest, and loyal Knight of the Royal Guard." Vladimir said softly.

When he looked up again he did not see a glimmer of fear on Olivia's face, just simple curiosity.

"So you are the Daemon Wolf that everyone is raving about." She said lightly moving to stand beside him. Vladimir was a little unnerved by her easy acceptance of him. But did not question it, in fact he was glad for the company, for the fact that for once that someone besides his father was not afraid of him. They started talking slowly and hesitantly Vladimir choosing his words wisely not wanting to frighten this young Vampiress off. When the party ended Vladimir escorted Lady Olivia to the door. Asking her to please come again as he genuinely enjoyed her company.

Volume One

Chapter Six

Those ten years with his father passed far too quickly, too soon for Vladimir. Vladimir met all Knights of the Royal Guard. They seemed to be honorable yet there was an underlying grittiness to them. These men and women were not afraid to get their hands dirty to do what needed to be done. As his father introduced Vladimir to each of the Knights Vladimir committed their names and grim faces to memory. He knew that possibly one day, from the looks of disgust that many of the Knights gave him, that he would have to defend himself from their blades. Or perhaps those looks of disgust were not directed at the fact that he was a half breed, but because he had not yet reached the full accepted level of maturity to be considered a functioning member of Immortal society.

Then again it could be both those reasons. The only Knight that seemed to like Vladimir was a withered shell of a man, a Vampire from the smell of him, though his eyes said differently, they flashed green in the light, his personal scent was light and airy, fresh like water. Vladimir's father introduced Vladimir to this man last.

"Vladimir this is Lord Aodhan the halfblooded, he is the son of Carmag the winter wolf and Mordag the daughter of King Drostan of the Isles." Vladimir looked at the withered man with respect, here was another half breed. A half breed that was far older than either his father or grandfather.

The man stood and crossed his arm over his breast plate. Looking pleased to have finally made Vladimir's acquaintance.

"Greetings Prince Vladimir Halfblooded, I have been waiting many a long year to meet you." Aodhan said lightly as he embraced Vladimir. Who was in shock that the man could actually move. He seemed so old and fragile. "Come we will have much to discuss before the end of the night, you may ask me any question." Aodhan said in a thick rolling drawl as he grasped Vladimir's shoulder in a deceptively strong grip and led him to a chair beside the fire. The first words out of Vladimir's mouth were.

"How old are you?" Aodhan laughed and grinned baring his fangs, showing them to be strong and firm.

"I was here when your grandfather took his throne, in fact I helped him take it which is a fact your grandfather forgets far too often." Aodhan said with a laugh his voice lowered as he said with a small smile. "He often forgets that it was my strength that put his behind on the throne, and it is my strength that can unseat him if I so desire." Vladimir shook his head as Aodhan leaned back in his seat.

"Then I will take your guidance old one." Vladimir said wisely. Aodhan laughed and reached out to slap Vladimir on the shoulder. "You will need more than guidance young one, if you want to survive the coming trials." He said lightly with a twinkle in his eye it was like he knew that he knew something that Vladimir did not. "I may command the Knights of the Royal Guard, but they do not follow my every wish, you will have to prove yourself to them and then some before you will truly be one of us."

Vladimir reported to Aodhan the following morning after his last night with his father. Aodhan welcomed him to the Knight's Headquarters warmly though the other Knights frowned at his arrival and shunned him openly. He knew the only way to be accepted was to gain their respect, was to be the most dangerous person in the room. His reputation had preceded him into the order, but it did little but give the other Knights, particularly the younger ones something to speculate about. He knew that when they had determined it as nothing more than myth then they would attack him. Vladimir was determined to prove it to them, he was truly the Daemon Wolf that everyone spoke of and that he was dangerous.

Aodhan led him to where he would be resting his head and left him to unpack. Vladimir looked around the small room and sighed, the first thing he unpacked was his Compendium which he wrote in for a few hours before finishing his unpacking and going to bed making sure that his door and windows were secured properly before doing so. One could never be too careful, and Vladimir had learned time and time again. His paranoia usually kept him alive.

    Dawn found Vladimir already up and dressed in the yard going through the forms with his sword. There was a crowd gathering around him as he practiced, some eyed him with envy, others with wary vigilance. Vladimir kept the routines simple; it would not do for him to betray all his secrets. It would not do for him to portray himself right out as a brilliant swordsman, the more he showed of himself the better measure his opponents would have of him. That was something that Vladimir did not want, he did not want a dagger planted in his back.

    He wanted them to think less of him to think him less of a threat. Vladimir smiled to himself as one of the older Knights drew their weapon and approached him. Aodhan was watching from the steps of the yard with a small smile on his face. He called out over the yard.

"Fifty coins says the Prince scores first blood." There were some scattered laughs through the yard and an upstart young Knight spat on the ground before declaring for the entire yard to hear.

"I'll double that bet old man, Riven will teach the Princeling a thing or two about the blade I bet he will have first blood." Vladimir looked his opponent over and lowered his sword tip as he assessed the threat the Knight posed to him.

The man was a hulking mass of muscle, larger than Vladimir, and from the glint of his eyes a Lycanthrope. Vladimir bowed his head to the man in respect and remained still as the man bellowed and charged at him. He did not even flinch as Riven charged in swinging his sword. Instead he fixed Riven with a cool glare, and watched as the man came to a labored halt not a foot from him. Sword raised high as if to strike, naturally one would assume that Riven had Vladimir, except for the expression of agony on Riven's face and the length of Vladimir's sword that impaled him up to the hilt through the gut. Vladimir gripped his sword hilt and withdrew the blade slowly as he stepped off to the side. He had raised his sword only in the last seconds of Riven's charge when the man was fully committed to his course and could not deviate from it.

    Riven gasped and fell to his knees his eyes rolling into the back of his head. The wound would not prove fatal, only a wound to the heart, or to the brain would kill an Immortal, destroy those two parts of the body and you destroyed the Immortal. Otherwise they healed to fast to die from most other wounds. Aodhan stood and walked across the yard to the impudent youth and held his hand out. The young Knight reluctantly counted out the coin. Aodhan pushed his way through the Knights collecting the coins in a large leather sack before coming to Vladimir and holding up the sack he said in his thick rolling drawl.

"The Princeling drew first blood, and he faced fierce Riven a true beast in battle without even flinching! Therefore this money is his fairly won, and I dare any one of you to try and take it from him by force." Aodhan stated putting the sack in

Vladimir's free hand and patting him on the shoulder as he walked out of the circle of outraged onlookers. Vladimir looked at the sack and guessed there had to be roughly a thousand coins in it.

    He could certainly do quite a bit with that money if he wanted to, but what was the point when he preferred to make whatever it was that he needed? His mother had taught him carving and carpentry; his father had taught him jewelry, and blacksmithing. Vladimir started away from the yard after wiping his sword on Riven's tunic as he passed. He returned to his room and locked the coins in the bottom of his chest, and yes he could do any number of things with that money. But he would instead add to it slowly, invest it into something worthwhile and watch it succeed as a business, but first he would need more money. That would mean following his orders and completing missions for Aodhan with the other Knights. If he moved up in the ranks, then his pay would increase. Vladimir had every intention of doing this and more in order to survive. He smiled to himself as he closed the lid of his chest and locked it.

    The first few days of living at the headquarters were tense to say the least of it. The other Knights either looked down at him in some manner or shunned him all together. Vladimir could not care less about the attitude that the other Knights showed towards him. As far as he was concerned they were just tools to his survival. He would use them as he could and throw them away when he no longer needed them. There was nothing more he needed from the other Knights than that, if he could earn their respect in the process then all the better.

    Aodhan was the only Knight that Vladimir trusted or even remotely respected, as the old man respected him to a degree even if the old man did not trust him. More to the point the old man could not trust him, as a member of the Royal family Aodhan could not trust him, could not trust who's side Vladimir would chose. His grandfathers or Aodhan's. Vladimir watched his surroundings carefully as the days passed him by; it was like he was back at the Academy. A constant edge of paranoia was creeping in on him as he settled into his daily life at the headquarters. He undertook his first few missions with ease. Completing them successfully and with a modicum of grace.

They were simple missions, escorting lower Nobles, locating thieves, and protecting important ladies. He was promoted by Aodhan not once but twice in rapid succession, then he was sent out into the field on longer missions maintaining the peace amongst the packs and outer covens that chose not to reside in the capital. Vladimir marched along with his comrades and followed orders to the letter and even beyond fulfilling his obligations and duties to his father and the crown.

This went on for several decades, five to be exact. Vladimir doing all that he could to survive and top the Knights in the order. Which he succeeded at, becoming a Knight Commander within a few short years, in those years he rarely returned to the Capital. But he did invest his growing wealth within Coelum and expanded his wealth quickly and efficiently after a couple of failed business ventures of course. Vladimir was diligent and intelligent, a quick learner but he still had to fail a few times before he got his successful enterprises running and bringing in coin even then there were losses that were to be expected from time to time. When he returned to Coelum, Vladimir never failed to pay a visit to Lady Olivia; she was one of the few friends that he had that he could trust.

  Aodhan quickly grew dear to him, almost as dear as a father; Aodhan taught Vladimir a number of things. The man taught him the value of friendship, kindness, and mercy, things that Vladimir had been lacking until then. Things that Vladimir hadn't thought were necessary. Aodhan also taught Vladimir the importance of hiding his vulnerabilities, helping Vladimir perfect it so that his enemies could not take advantage of him. A few of the older Knights that were somewhat more at ease with Vladimir as they had spent most of their lives with Aodhan, taught him about lust. About the pleasures the bodies of men and women could hold.

Vladimir was patrolling with his group in the northern boundaries in the summer of his eighty-sixth year of life, when they received a message by hawk, as the reigning Knight Commander. Vladimir was the first to read the missive. And his heart fell as he read it. There was an official declaration that went with the missive.

Knight Commander Vladimir you are to take your regiment and quell an uprising twenty miles from the Northern Boundary, approximately thirty miles from your base camp to the east and another ten miles to the North. None of these traitors are to be spared. Go with speed by the Emperors will. Do not fail in this task.

Vladimir growled to himself and tucked the missive and the declaration into his belt pouch. "Form up, we're moving out." Vladimir snapped to his forty some Knights pulling his equipment up and onto his shoulders. He checked his sword and pulled out a map of the area. It was highly detailed and he quickly found the little village that the missive was referring to.

It was a mixed community, both Vampires and Lycanthropes. Vladimir formulated a plan of attack; if the village was truly participating in an uprising then they would be expecting an invasion from the roads which was the easiest way into the village. He understood what he had to do, what he was being ordered to do. This was genocide pure and simple. Vladimir laid out his battle plan and explained it to his Knights; many of them were younger than him by a few years, so they listened without question. The older ones knew better by now then to question his authority.

"Remember spare no one, but keep it tight and clean I want no loses on our side, you are not to loot or pillage." Vladimir said softly to his men as they got into formation. "I find any of you did and I will personally reeve your head from your shoulders myself." He growled to them as each of them crossed their fists over their breast plates and Vladimir started them out at a quick pace.

It took them the better part of two days to get into position, Vladimir did not want to take any chances so he let his men take their time, he did not rush them. Once they were in position, Vladimir crept down to the village to scope out the resistance they would be encountering. The villagers were in light armor and armed to the teeth. The roads were blocked off and even the cubs looked on edge. Vladimir growled to himself and made his way back to his troops. As the sun began its descent he gave the order to attack, leading the charge into the startled village militia himself. Screams rent the air and blood splattered the dirt as Vladimir led his Knights into the fray, the villagers never had a chance.

  Vladimir wanted to close his eyes, to deny the horror that was unfolding before him. But it was his voice that was barking the commands that sent his Knights into each of the houses searching for more of the villagers; it was his voice that barked the order that ended those lives. Vladimir could see clearly the frightened eyes of the children as they pleaded for mercy. He gave them that mercy, a quick clean death, they never saw it coming. Vladimir saw the disgust in his companion's eyes as they looked at him, he could see himself reflected in their eyes and he was a terrible sight to behold. Armor coated in the blood of innocent children, his eyes lit with an inner light, almost glowing of their own accord, and his face blank expressionless like there was not a thing in the world wrong with what he had done.

    The truth was far from that Vladimir was horrified with what he had done, he wanted nothing more than to cast his sword from him, shed his armor and shift his shape and run just to run from this. But he could not this blood would never wash from his hands or his soul. Vladimir looked around at the devastation around him and pointed to the nearest of buildings and ordered his men to burn it. Burn it all, he said coldly. It was the only burial that he could give the villagers that would be accepted by his grandfather.

    Vladimir watched the village burn from a cliff not far off in the forest, beside him a river plunged off the cliff face in a majestic water fall, beneath the cliff face was a lake where his

Knights bathed and discussed the battle amongst themselves almost eagerly; Vladimir was disgusted with them, with himself. Even from this height Vladimir could hear the conversations keenly. The main topic of discussion was him.

"…Can't believe he actually killed the children…" one young Knight said to an older one, the older one scoffed and dunked the younger one's head under water.

"…Careful what you say, the Daemon Wolf could hear you and decide your head will be next for the block…" the older one said as the younger one came up. The eldest of the group snarled and pointed to the cliff and said.

"…You think he has a choice of which orders he follows? I bet his orders are explicit, he is a Prince of the Royal family, and what's worse he is a half breed; they are just looking for an excuse to execute him…" Vladimir smiled he had at least garnered the respect and admiration of one of his group.

"…Yeah but that doesn't mean he has to enjoy his work so much…" another one cut in.

Vladimir shook out his hair and took a few steps back before launching himself off the face of the cliff, he was still in armor, but the rest of his gear was still up on the cliff. As much as he wanted to deny their words, he knew that if he did and his grandfather learned of it. He would be signing the death warrants of himself and his mother.

    He spun through the air gracefully, before he pierced the water like an arrow shot from a bow. Vladimir sank right to the bottom of the lake and he pushed off the slimy bottom with his boots, swimming powerfully for the surface. When he breached the surface of the cool water he was faced with forty stunned faces, he looked up at the cliff and shrugged, he hadn't realized that it was that high. Water and blood ran off him in rivulets staining the water around him red. Vladimir swam towards the water fall and climbed on top of a rock underneath it and began to scrub himself. When he was done he stripped out of his armor and clothes and scrubbed them till they were clean. He then dipped back into the lake and scrubbed himself again. When he was clean and his clothes were dry he donned them again and donned his armor. He went back up the cliff to fetch his equipment and scaled back down again to lead his men back to the sight of where the village once stood.

    He had them cut down a decent sized tree, strip it of its branches and sink it halfway up its trunk into the ground, he found a long nail and pinned the declaration up to the post. When he left the ruined village with his men he left haunted with the screams of the dying, and worse yet, the screams of the children.

Volume One

Chapter Seven

Nearly ten years passed in this manner Vladimir passed his ninety-sixth year and was now known by a new name Lord Daemon, the Daemon wolf and it was a name well-earned as he had earned it in the Academy, then again as a Royal Knight fulfilling his duties. Not to mention what he did to would be assassins. It was not a name he had chosen as of yet. But it was a name that was used in place of his real name when others were discussing him. Even Aodhan used it as he jested with Vladimir, and Lady Olivia used it often as an endearing term. Vladimir hardly cared what name he was addressed by, he knew who he was. He was a Knight of the Royal Guard a Commander at that, a Prince of the Royal house, and the son of the most powerful and respected Alpha in all the Northern provinces.

Vladimir was writing in his Compendium when there was a knock on his door. When he opened it he was surprised to see Aodhan standing there looking rather agitated and in a foul mood, dressed in a hooded cloak as if he needed secrecy. Aodhan came in quickly and closed the door and slapped a letter down on Vladimir's desk. Vladimir looked at what remained of the Royal seal that was on it and looked at Aodhan who was all but heaving with anger.

"My orders." Aodhan explained curtly, motioning for Vladimir to read. Vladimir went to the desk and opened the folded parchment and read the flowing script on the page carefully.

Grandmaster Knight Aodhan Halfblooded, you are to here by to carry out the execution of Prince Vladimir otherwise known as Lord Daemon as he has become a danger to the throne. You are then to send a detachment to the village that harbors the Lady Shadow and you are to destroy all evidence that she and the village ever existed. This is the will of your Emperor, good speed.

It was signed by the Emperors own hand, not the hand of any of the Council of Ten from whom most of the Knights orders came from. Vladimir recognized his grandfather's handwriting and signature having seen it once before, on a declaration condemning the first village that Vladimir had sent into oblivion.

Aodhan sighed as Vladimir sank into his chair in shock. He ran his hands through his hair and spoke softly to Vladimir.

"I have already sent out the detachment, but I have one last thing I must do before you go to face them." Aodhan pulled Vladimir's face around to face him. "This is the greatest gift I can give you and it will help you defeat your grandfather." Vladimir looked at him confused. Aodhan smiled and bared his fangs.

"My body is too frail to wield the strength that I have, so I have come to give it to you, this is something only those with Ancient blood can do." Aodhan said softly. "As I have said before it was my strength that put your family on the throne, it is my strength that will unseat them but it will not be me who wields it." Vladimir nodded he understood, he understood that this was indeed a great gift.

But he was not so foolish to think that it would not come without great cost. He knew instinctively that this was going to kill Aodhan.

Normally an Immortal could not be killed unless their head or hearts were damaged, that was the general rule. But if you can drain an Immortal of their life's blood then they will die, a hard feat to do unless you are an Ancient or a Vampire of great strength and age. Vladimir nodded to Aodhan and bared his fangs, Aodhan did not resist, and he did not flinch as Vladimir's fangs dug into his flesh.

    The taste of Aodhan's blood was indescribable, the old man stiffened as Vladimir drank deeply, taking Aodhan into himself, because with the blood came a rush of memories and strength that was not his own. It was not so much physical strength, as it was strength of will and knowledge, the knowledge about himself, what he was, what Aodhan was, what his grandfather Victor was, how Aodhan thought and all the knowledge of his years and dealings with Vladimir's grandfather and various others. With every draught Vladimir grew stronger and Aodhan grew weaker, and Vladimir experienced Aodhan's life. Vladimir listened to the shuddering of Aodhan's heart and continued to drink until there was nothing left and Aodhan's heart came to a shuddering halt.

Vladimir laid the old man down and wiped the remnants of the blood off his lips. He thought quickly, using not only his own memories, perhaps Aodhan's body could serve as a cover to get him out of the capital. They were of the same height and weight approximately he could lay Aodhan in his bed and flee Coelum to go after the detachment that was going after his mother and her pack. Vladimir carefully covered Aodhan and gathered his things mainly his money and his sword he would need both before the end. His Compendium was a must; he would not part with it on his life, not unless he could find a safe place for it. Other than that he needed nothing.

He wrote a quick letter to Lady Olivia, explaining the situation. Before he slipped a cloak around his shoulders, and pulling the hood up over his face he strode out of the room. Looking very much like Aodhan had when he had entered the room earlier. Vladimir handed the letter off to one of the pages downstairs and paid him to deliver the letter before disappearing into the night.

    Thanks to Aodhan's memories he knew what paths the detachment was taking to get to the village that held his mother and her pack, and with his new strength Vladimir made good time shifting to an in-between form that allowed him to travel on all fours but still allowed him to remain armored and clothed. In his head Aodhan's memories pounded him relentlessly, giving him new knowledge and experiences. It took three days for Vladimir to catch up to the detachment of Knights sent to wipe out his mother and her pack.

    And when he came upon them in his half form he lived up to the name he had been given. He was a vengeful demon as he set upon them, his sword was bright and his fangs gleamed as they tore into the Knights like a whirlwind of destruction, by the end of it his claws and fangs had done more damage than his sword, though his sword was dripping with the blood of his enemies. When every one of the fifty Knights lay dead Vladimir sheathed his sword and continued on his way, running full tilt towards his mother.

It took Vladimir almost a year to reach his mother's village in this manner and when he arrived he found it in chaos, the village was burning Vladimir immediately sorted out the problem there was an overabundance of Knights here, there should not have been any Knights here, he had killed the detachment that had been sent. But these Knights were mounted; on good steeds that was the only way they could have over taken him and even then just barely, the only person he had told that he would be intercepting the first detachment was Olivia. Had she betrayed him? Vladimir immediately set into the Knights attacking the village and began his swath of devastation.

He was still in his shifted form, so he was fast, agile and armed naturally to the teeth. Blood matted his fur and a red haze clouded Vladimir's vision but he was still in enough control to understand when the battle was over, he roared his victory sending horses skittering away from him and drawing concerned and confused glances from the villagers not a single one of them recognized him. By scent or by sight, so he must truly look like a stranger or an utter beast to them. He sorted through the mess of villagers and found his mother. Just as he saw an Knight with a Commander's helm creep up behind her to strike her down. Vladimir's body was in motion before he even registered the fact that his mother was in danger. His goal was not to kill the Knight but to scare him into submission; he wanted to know if Olivia had betrayed him.

    Vladimir flew past his mother and caught the Knight by his throat hoisting the man off the ground and roared baring his fangs to the fullest extent. The Knight growled back and bared his fangs in response, Vladimir recognized the Knight as the Knight he had impaled on his first day at the headquarters, Riven. Vladimir leveled his sword at the Knight and growled letting his features shift enough for him to speak.
"Who gave you the information that the other detachment had been intercepted?" Vladimir growled angrily. The Knight refused to answer

even as Vladimir brought the sword to bear on him, cutting a thick line in the man's throat. "Answer me fool." He snarled bringing the sword back so that he could swing again. The Knight flinched and gasped a name and Vladimir's heart plummeted.

"...Lady Olivia, it was Lady Olivia that told us that the other regiment had been waylaid." Vladimir snarled and ended the Knight with a swift strike to the heart.

    He turned to his mother who was watching him warily, like she did not recognize him. Vladimir knelt and touched his fingers to his lips then to his brow in a gesture of respect. Surely he had matured over the years but not enough that she would recognize her own son. He looked up as his mother fell to her knees beside him.

"Tá tú ag teacht abhaile." *You have come home.* Vladimir rested his head on his mother's shoulder feeling the pain of his injuries.

"Níl sé ar fáil mháthair fada…" *Not for long mother.* Vladimir responded slowly, he stood and helped his mother to her feet. "You have to go, you have to get your pack to safety, find somewhere safe to hide and lay low for a while I have something to settle with my grandfather." Vladimir growled to her as he looked around at the remnants of her pack.

    The children had thankfully made it through, thanks to the sacrifices of their parents. Vladimir looked over his wounds and sighed; many of them were deep and bleed freely. They would take some time to heal he would have to go into hiding until they healed. His mother frowned at him and brushed his hair out of his face.

"Your scent has changed, its deeper, older than it should be." She said softly worriedly, Vladimir smiled and spread his arms out wide.

"Níl mé an fear céanna a d'fhág an sráidbhaile tríocha dó bliain ó shin tá mé Prionsa Vladimir an mac tíre daemon." *I am not the same man that left this village eighty-one years ago; I am Prince Vladimir, the Daemon Wolf.* Vladimir declared crossing his arm over his breast. "I am Lord Daemon Mac Tíre, and I will stop at nothing until I end the threat to my existence."

He swore his mother took a step back her face perplexed by what she saw in him in that moment. She saw a man both honorable and proud, but at the same time she saw a killer, a stone cold killer that would not hesitate to kill any and all that got in his way. This was a man who had blood on his hands, blood that would never wash off.

    Vladimir watched as his mother organized her remaining pack members and got them ready to go. He had seen in his mother's eyes fear as she looked at him, but not fear of him, fear for him. For what he had become, Vladimir smiled to himself; there was no amount of atonement in this world he could ever achieve that would wash him clean. It would be best to give up on that thought before he even began thinking along that path.

    What he had done was something that he could never ask forgiveness for, it was something that he would never forgive himself for doing. Because he could have run away, he could have hid until the time was right. Vladimir did not think of anything past that and he grabbed a horse and spurred it in the direction of his father's castle. If anyone deserved a fair warning in what was coming then it would be his father. Besides Vladimir thought it would be best if he at least eluded his plans to his father instead of just springing them on his father.

He pushed the horse until the horse collapsed from exhaustion, and then he continued to run on his own in his shifted shape overtaking miles and leagues. Days flew past him as he drew closer to his goal he slowed down, slipping in and out of populated areas to listen to the rumors. Most of them were pretty wild, but the general talk spoke that the Crown Prince had been confined to his castle on house arrest, the Grandmaster of the Knights of the Royal Guard had been found slain in the chambers of a lesser Knight, and that the Lady Shadow had started an uprising in the north but no one can find her or her pack. Vladimir growled and found that wanted posters of himself had been plastered up in all the towns and villages across Athartha, at least all the ones that he had visited so far, mortal and immortal alike. It gave a general description though nothing useful, but it was offering a substantial reward for any Lycanthrope matching the description.

    Vladimir had the makings of a full beard that hid most of his face and his hair was long and ragged. The description was for someone who would keep to a strict military haircut and protocol. Vladimir was not that stupid, breaking his regimented habits was probably what saved his life on more than one occasion. Along with the fact that he had killed most every Knight that knew what he looked like. Aodhan had probably planned it that way letting Vladimir fall upon his former close comrades that fateful day that Aodhan had given Vladimir his strength. These Knights that now patrolled the streets were novices to the Knighthood. None of them were the ones that had been around Vladimir long enough to study his face because unless it was his own regiment of Knights or the rare few that actually tolerated Vladimir none would know his face. Vladimir had rarely socialized with the other Knights of the Guard.

It helped too, now that five years had passed since the Emperor had issued his execution order. The Knights were getting lax as time wore on. Vladimir slipped up to the gate of his father's castle and vaulted over it. It was easy to sneak in despite the increased security. Vladimir did not know if it was his own skill or the lack thereof with the men guarding his father's home. He found his father in his study and slipped in leaving the two Guards outside dead and pinned to the wall by their own swords. His father looked him over and scowled. "You should not be here, it is dangerous." He said softly, Vladimir bowed his head and scratched at his beard unconcernedly. It had been rather easy to slip in, so it must not have been so dangerous.

"Not so dangerous as you might think, I came to warn you that I will be ending grandfather's life and the lives of the Council of Ten." Vladimir said softly in return, his father looked at him shocked.

"You intend to take the throne?" he asked incredulously, Vladimir growled and shook his head.

"I have no plans of ascending to the throne before you do; I am simply going to do what you haven't been able to do." Vladimir stated slowly. "I intend to end the tyranny of my grandfather and the tyranny of that damned Council of Ten that is all." His father ran a hand through his hair and came to wrap him in a tight embrace; his father stepped back and rubbed his face roughly.

  They stared at each other for a long moment, neither willing to speak the words they both needed to hear. After a long while Vladimir's father spoke again. Reluctantly giving his son his blessing to do what needed to be done.

"Vladimir, you will do what you think is right and no one can fault you that." His father stated slowly. "My father does deserve to die for what he has done, and it saddens me that it must be you that has to do this deed for I cannot, I do not have the strength of spirit that you possess nor the depth of faith in myself." Vladimir pulled further away and put his Compendium on the desk. He gave his father a small smile as he tapped it gently with his forefinger.

"I am entrusting this to you for the time being, when I return I will want to finish it." Vladimir said lightly. His father smiled and touched the worn leather face of the book.

"You only have a few pages left in it, I'll see to it that another Compendium is made for your return, I am sure you will have more to write than you think." His father stated calmly like they were discussing everyday business. Vladimir bared his fangs and bowed his head to his father and slipped out of the castle like a shadow in the night.

  Vladimir returned to the capital, after three decades. As he had to plan his return in detail and let the heat die down. He had to remain unnoticed in a city on full alert for his presence. He learned over the course of a few weeks that his businesses had been seized and shut down, currently the buildings were abandoned. Vladimir flitted from building to building using each one as a sanctuary in its own as he laid out his plan of attack. Using his knowledge of the palace and some of the blueprints from the Grand City Library Vladimir solidified his plan over the course of several months. He was of course willing and prepared to do a lot of on the fly thinking and preparation using not only his knowledge but Aodhan's as well.

When the time drew nigh for him to begin his attack Vladimir bought a mirror, washed himself thoroughly in a public bathhouse before retreating to one of his sanctuaries to shave and cut his hair. He wanted his grandfather to recognize him, it was a little self-serving but he wanted his grandfather's last image to be him. Vladimir tied his sword to his belt and walked out into Coelum.

Not one city guard paid him any attention, not even the Knights standing at the corners. Vladimir pushed on through to the palace where security was tighter and he was sure to be recognized. He made it past the first few steps without being challenged by the Royal Knights that were stationed there. But a young Knight Commander loomed up before him and barked. "What'd be yer business at the palace sir?" Vladimir looked at the youth from under his lashes and smiled. He was unknown to this young Knight, as he was undoubtedly unknown to many of the others.

If any of them knew him or guessed who he was they wisely kept their mouths shut. "I am on official business with the Emperor whelp; step down before I put you down boy." Vladimir growled to the youth, who could not have been more than a couple of years younger than Vladimir was but Vladimir needed to prove he was the dominant one of the two and did indeed belong in the palace by the Emperors side. The youth was astounded and backed off almost immediately, apologizing profusely as he did so. Vladimir mounted the stairs and headed inside without hesitating or waiting for the youth to gather his courage again to question him more closely.

Following the blue prints that he had taken from the library and committed to memory, Vladimir made his way to his grandfather's private quarters. The man would not likely be there at this time of day. But there was something that Vladimir had to do before he carried out his plan. Something that Aodhan's memories and instincts guided him to do. Creeping into his grandfather's study he went straight up to the desk and pulled a fresh piece of parchment towards him along with a sample of the Emperor's handwriting. Forgery was a skill that Aodhan happened to be quite adept at, and now that Vladimir had absorbed Aodhan's essence it was something that even Vladimir could do with efficiency. Vladimir wrote many decrees, one ending the hunt for the Lady Shadow and her pack and clearing her of all charges, another ending the imprisonment of his father, one dissolving the Council of Ten, and only as a last thought did he think to write a decree that cleared him of all charges against him.

    How would he be able to help his father ascend to the throne if he was killed because of a silly misunderstanding? He stamped them all with the Royal seal, placed them in a leather satchel and carried them out of the living quarters. Quickly he found a page and paid him the remaining amount of his coin to deliver the missives. Thinking better of his attack now that he had lingered to long Vladimir slipped back out of the palace and resumed his waiting.

Volume One

Chapter Eight

Vladimir waited until he heard for a fact that his father was in the Coelum, it was some months later and the capital was still in an uproar over the declarations of innocence of his mother and of himself. But none of the decrees had been reversed, perhaps because they wanted to lure Vladimir into a trap. Make him think that he had gotten away with it. Vladimir was not that stupid.

He had allowed his beard to grow again and had taken up work at a tavern and inn that was frequented by Knights of the Royal Guard. It was a dangerous ploy but it was the only way that he could get information for free and spread a little rumor of his own while he was at it. Once Vladimir was sure that his father was in the capital and was residing in the palace he reformulated his plan of attack. He felt restless and on edge. It had been a full year since he had been in the palace; it was time to end this.

This time his attack route lie mainly in stealth, he did not need to get into his grandfather's chambers, he just needed to find his father and his grandfather in the same room together. He trusted his grandfather would send the Guards away so that he could have a private chat with his son. After trimming his beard and hair. Vladimir waited until dusk to creep into the palace and navigated his way to the throne room, which doubled as the dining room when the Emperor had guests. Vladimir encountered very few Guards on his way in. Vladimir gripped his sword tightly as he prowled through the shadows of the corridors getting closer to his goal with every step.

  The throne room had five potential entrances and exits, two to the left and two to the right and the main entrance. The main entrance had four Guards outside and it was through here that Vladimir entered slaughtering the four Guards without hesitation. He pushed the doors open and entered the throne room where his father and grandfather waited.

  His grandfather was sitting at the head of a magnificent mahogany table, fork stopped halfway to his mouth as his eyes were locked on

Vladimir in the same look of abject disgust that he had on the day he had Knighted Vladimir. As Vladimir closed the door his father mumbled something and Vladimir bowed and came to the table. Keeping in mind that despite his plans to kill the fool, his grandfather was still the emperor. Thus he needed to respect him, for he was a great warrior in his own right.

"Sorry I am late grandfather, father. I misplaced my invitation it seems." Vladimir stated softly shaking the blood off his hands as he came to a stop a few feet away from the far end of the table. His grandfather slowly lowered his fork back down to the table.

"I do not recall inviting a mongrel to dine with me." He said roughly, Vladimir smiled back at him and showed his fangs.

His hand was tight on his sword and he tapped the blood stained blade against his leg lightly.

"To be honest I did not come here for the meal grandfather, I came here to end your life." Vladimir said coldly, his grandfather cocked his head to the side and scoffed. Vladimir leveled his sword at his grandfather and dropped it with a ringing clatter onto the table. He felt the heat of the change wash down his spine, and grinned eagerly. He could feel Aodhan's strength in his limbs, and it calmed him some to know that even though his friend was gone, he was still there to support him.

    His grandfather stood and stepped away from the table and drew a long wickedly sharp sword from a sheath at his belt. Vladimir's grin widened as he eyed the sword, he was not wearing any armor, but he was confident he could end this before his grandfather could put that sword through his heart or took his head. "Will you face me with just your claws and fangs boy or are you going to pick up that fine blade and down me with it?" his grandfather asked lightly, confidently. There was no inclination in his grandfathers bearing that he thought anything else then Vladimir would lose to him.

    Vladimir rolled his head on his shoulders and stepped away from the table. Flexing his fingers Vladimir smiled and responded with a chuckle.

"I do not need a sword to beat you." Vladimir said as the change took him over completely taking his features and shifting them into a half form giving him the head and fur of a wolf and the body of a man. His nails extended into claws and a tail sprouted as he snarled viciously his eyes fixed on his grandfather. Vision blurring and going red Vladimir licked his chops wickedly. His grandfather looked him over and swung his sword a few times, the man did not look any less confident or any more intimidated than a man scolding a disobedient child.

The motion of the sword cutting through air was quick and precise. Vladimir nodded as he scented the air, his grandfather exuded confidence and nothing but. He roared as he completed the change and started forward. All he needed was to get a hold of his grandfather; he had Aodhan's strength on his side, all of Aodhan's wisdom and fighting experience. After that nothing else mattered once he got a hold of his grandfather and latched on with his fangs there would be little that could throw him off. Vladimir growled as his grandfather's blade sliced into him again and again. But the wounds were not serious and he was able to get in close it was obvious that his grandfather did not take this seriously.

They danced around each other for several minutes each taking measured swipes and at their opponent. Before actually engaging for a few seconds in a furious exchange of blows that left both of them with nicks and cuts when they disengaged. Vladimir licked at a wound on his hand with a sly smile admiring how red his grandfather's blood was against the white of the marble floor. They engaged again and exchanged another furious encounter in which Vladimir almost got a hold of his grandfather and nearly got his fangs to bear, but his grandfather brought his sword slicing across Vladimir's belly slicing him from hip to shoulder.

Vladimir hissed and backed away quickly one hand against the deepest part of the wound. He looked at his grandfather and snarled angrily. His rage was building to a boiling point and it was getting hard to ignore, but he could see on his grandfather's face the irritation and the confusion as to why Vladimir was still alive. Vladimir smirked as much as his wolfish face would allow and put his every effort into dazzling and throwing his grandfather off his guard so that he could finish this fight, so that he could put an end to this once and for all.

Vladimir feinted to his left and left his side open deliberately leaving himself open. These last few moments of this fight he thought he had figured out his grandfather. If he gave his grandfather an opening, just maybe, just maybe his grandfather would take it and give him the advantage. It was a simple trick, something that a novice should have been aware of, and something that a man who had been fighting for almost six hundred years shouldn't fall far.

Unless that man was prideful, arrogant, and thought that Vladimir really was that stupid and beneath him. His grandfather jabbed out with the sword and Vladimir accepted it letting the blade drive deep into his side as he grabbed hold of his grandfather. Vladimir did not hesitate to drive his fangs through the soft flesh of his grandfather's throat and begin to drink his form shifting to his normal human semblance as he did so. His grandfather fought, with every ounce of his being realizing that this was no longer a simple fight for superiority; this was a fight to the death and had always had been from the very beginning. But it was to no avail against the combined might of both the younger Vladimir and the elder essence of Aodhan.

    Vladimir growled as he drained his grandfather dry, the taste of his grandfather's blood was beyond foul in his mouth. It made him sick to his stomach but he kept drinking even after the man's attempts to gain freedom grew feeble then nonexistent. Slowly his grandfather stopped moving altogether, his heartbeat shuddering in Vladimir's ears.

    Vladimir continued to drink until he heard that heart beat its very last beat. When it had he dropped his grandfather's corpse at his feet and turned to his father, pulling his grandfather's blade from his gut as he did so. Vladimir dropped to one knee before his father and raised his voice so that the guards outside the room that were still alive could hear.

"Hail Emperor Vladimir the first." From the other four exits a dozen or so Knights poured into the room, they immediately went for Vladimir, but released him when his father snarled at them. Vladimir returned to his kneeling position and reiterated his earlier words. Slowly and with shocked looks the Knights followed his example and knelt before their new Emperor. Vladimir knew he would have to silence them one way or the another before long.

    Vladimir did not stay long in the Coelum; he fought bitterly with his father about who was the real Emperor. He denied that the right was his, saying vehemently that his father should take the throne as he would be a much better ruler than him. In the end his father took the throne reluctantly but with grace. Vladimir took off after the ten Ancients that governed the Council of Ten finding them where ever they were hiding. One by one he challenged them and defeated them, he refrained from absorbing their essences though, as he had already tasted one Immortal that had been corrupted beyond retribution and had not enjoyed the drink, besides he already had Aodhan's essence who had been seven hundred and ninety three years old to start with, and his grandfather who was six hundred and some odd years old and who had absorbed the strength of his predecessors and the line of Kings before that.

There was no need to further his power at this moment; he was one of the strongest Immortals alive and probably the most determined to survive. The hunting of the Council took approximately a decade. Vladimir returned to the Coelum one last time before heading to the site of where his estate would sit. His father had a proposition for him since he had declined his rightful place on the throne. Vladimir would take a position of great power and authority in the Empire, it would place him in command of the Knights of the Royal Guard and of men of his own choosing. His task would be simple, to hunt down and punish any and all who broke his father's laws. Vladimir was more than willing to accept this position, he was in fact eager to begin. He saw it as an opportunity to do good with his position and power, and he was sure to do a thorough job before declaring anyone guilty of a crime.

    His stay in the Coelum was rather long as his father had to officially declare the position and hold court to notarize the position with the court Nobles before he could ordain Vladimir into the position before the entire upper and lower Courts. Besides that Vladimir had some unfinished business to take care of with the Lady Olivia. His closest friend and the woman he had been considering for a partnership for life had betrayed him. He wanted to know her reasons for doing so, he thought that if he knew her reasons then perhaps that he could forgive her and they could continue their friendship, if not their courtship as he would not continue courting a woman he could not trust with his life.

    The day before his ordaining and swearing in Vladimir went to see Lady Olivia having needed that long to convince himself that he did indeed want to see her face to face. He found her in her home 'entertaining' several guests. Vladimir was not surprised to see this; this was nothing less than Olivia's typical behavior. Patiently he waited in the doorway for Olivia to notice him before approaching her slowly and carefully like she was a viper that could bite him if he handled her wrong. He snapped a glare on the men she was with and growled.

"Leave us." Making them flee for safety. Vladimir took a seat on the settee and leaned forward as he fixed Olivia with his cold glaring gaze.

Her expression was one of bemusement and simple curiosity. His words were simple and cut straight to the point.

"Why did you betray me to the Knights?" Olivia scoffed rolling her eyes and leaned back against her plush cushions and waved her hand through the air dismissively like she did not believe he had just asked that.

"What is the general motivation Lord Daemon? Power, fortune, fame, the ability to go to the Emperor and say I was the one who had that information and gave it willingly how will you reward me?" She said in a matter of fact tone like this was an everyday thing and the saddest part of it was that it was true; most Immortals bothered themselves with nothing more than their own skins.

Vladimir nodded and snapped a glare on her that would have shriveled the bravest of men. He knew now what motivated her, and he wanted nothing to do with her any more.
"You should know that I would never have betrayed you the way you did me; I would never have betrayed you regardless of the circumstances." Vladimir stated as he stood. He turned to leave and as he reached the door he looked over his shoulder and said. "I have realized as we have talked that you never were my friend, I do not want you to come near me, I do not want you to ever talk to me again beyond what civility requires." He walked out the door and slammed it shut behind him, making the entire wall shudder and breaking a few panes of stained glass in the process.

Waiting impatiently in his room of the palace Vladimir dressed in his best and got ready for the coming ceremony. His father had crafted him a new set of armor just for this occasion, a silver and gold breast plate, bracers,

Volume One

and boots. The gold inlay made patterns of knotted forests and wolves, with a snarling wolf head in the center of Vladimir's breast plate. At Vladimir's waist was his sword, held up by a thick, embossed leather belt clasped by a wolfs head belt buckle. Across Vladimir's chest was a crimson sash decorated with many shinning medals and accolades and on his brow was a gold circlet which held back his wavy ebony hair. Vladimir paced around his chamber and returned constantly to his desk to where his new Compendium lay. His father had expanded the volume of the book by at least three fold the original, his father had not forgotten to add the family tree. A tree to which Vladimir would add to when he found himself a suitable mate and raised himself a family.

But that was still a long way off, a future Vladimir currently could not see for himself. A family would be a weakness he could ill afford at this time. There was a knock on his door and Vladimir went to answer it, he bowed to his father's current advisor, a sprightly young page who had proven himself both wise and efficient.

Volume One

The man had been turned when he was already an old man though he was quite young for an Immortal. So his appearance was that of an Immortal beyond his years. Though in fact the man had only been an Immortal less than a year.

In fact, it was amazing this man had even survived the change. Given his advanced age at the time of his turning. Still though Vladimir respected the man a great deal. The man had skills Vladimir only dreamed of.
"Kain, is it time?" Vladimir asked slowly, watching the man warily, this man had been a legendary assassin as a mortal man. The man, Kain, bowed and nodded his head motioning with hand for Vladimir to follow him.
"Yes Lord Daemon, it is time, your father the Emperor is waiting for you in the throne room." Kain said lightly as he led the way through the palace to where Vladimir would take his place at his father's side as Crown Prince and his father's Regent, the keeper of his father's laws.

Kain entered the room first to announce Vladimir to the awaiting room of court nobles,

Kain's voice boomed out through the long hall. Vladimir was surprised that the thin man's voice could be so deep and loud, it was usually so whipish and sharp, and it really defied his size and soft voice.

"Announcing Crown Prince Vladimir Daemon Mac Tíre, son of Emperor Vladimir." Vladimir waited five seconds then entered the room at a slow dignified walk.

    He walked through a double line of Knights saluting him with drawn swords and to where his father was standing; when he reached there he knelt bowing his head reverently. His father touched his head lightly and Vladimir looked up, paying closer attention to who was standing beside his father, to his father's right was Vladimir's mother looking resplendent in the finery that she was owed as the Empress of night, a title that she had long deserved though officially she had to wait the traditional two decades for her coronation. To his left was a thin man holding a cushion with a gold and silver crown on it along with a signet ring. Vladimir paid little attention to these as they were ceremonial objects of his position as Crown Prince and Regent. He paid more attention to his father and the words he was saying. They were speaking in the old tongue, the guttural language spoken by the Immortals from time immemorial.

    The first order of business was his oaths of loyalty as the Crown Prince.
"Do you Vladimir hereby swear to forsake all other duties save the duties you hold to your people as their Prince?" His father asked him coldly. Vladimir looked him dead in the eye and answered back calmly.
"I swear on my life that I will put the people before myself, I will hold true to the duties and responsibilities of being the Crown Prince in times of war and in times of peace." Vladimir swore. His father gave him a small smile before continuing with a stern tone.
"Do you Prince Vladimir swear to take up the sword in defense of your people, to lay your life down for their sake?" his father asked Vladimir did not hesitate to answer.

"I would gladly lay down my life for my people, and in defense of them I shall raise my sword to meet the blood of their foes." Vladimir swore. His father nodded and smiled widely.

"Then I proclaim you Crown Prince and award you with all the rights and benefits of that title." His father said taking the crown off the cushion and placing it on Vladimir's head.

His father took the ring off the cushion and showed it to the entire room. Before saying in a deadly calm voice that had the entire room go still.

"Crown Prince Vladimir, I lay unto you the Title of Regent and Keeper of Law." He looked up at the crowd and spoke mostly to them, like he was warning them. "Do you Crown Prince Vladimir accept this title and all the responsibilities that it entails?" Vladimir looked up at his father and gave him a wolfish grin.

"I accept all duties and responsibilities that it entails." Vladimir said lightly, his father raised his voice and continued.

"Do you swear to uphold the law of the land and punish those that break those laws to the fullest extent of your abilities and what you deem is fair?" his father asked, Vladimir responded without a second of hesitation.

"I swear that I will uphold all the laws of the land to my fullest ability, I swear to pursue those that break the laws and punish them fairly and justly to the furthest extent of my ability." Vladimir swore coldly. His father shivered visibly and slid the ring onto the ring finger of Vladimir's right hand.

"Then I name you Regent and Keeper of Law, rise Crown Prince Vladimir, Emperor's Regent and face your people." Vladimir stood and faced the court Nobles with a hand on the pommel of his sword, eyes staring out coldly as he swept the audience.

    He caught a glimpse of Olivia, their eyes met and then he passed her over like she was just another noble Lady in the crowd. The hurt in her eyes did not bring Vladimir any pleasure but he did acknowledge it and quickly rejected all thought of Olivia being remorseful for her actions. Olivia was not that kind of person, she would never be remorseful over anything let alone something that had brought her much enjoyment and status. Vladimir found a reason to excuse himself from the party early and headed out for his estate.

Volume One

Chapter Nine

Fifty years passed since the day Vladimir left his father in the capital to rule, in that time Vladimir had raised himself a modest estate and helped the human village that stood not far off from his land flourish and grow by bringing in trade and making alliances with the human that ruled over the village. In this time Vladimir allowed Aodhan and his grandfather's essences to bleed into his own, he did not forcibly separate Aodhan and his grandfather's consciousness's from his own, he let them bleed together with his own and create a singularly unique individual, something new and dangerous.

He was not just Vladimir, he was Aodhan, he was his grandfather, but he was also none of them he was something else entirely. Making him a singularly deadly opponent, making him even more so into a cunning and vicious predator, at least on the surface. That was not all that made up Vladimir's new character, he was bound by a strict set of morals that he would not sway from. And in his private moments with the few whom he trusted Vladimir revealed himself to be kind, generous, considerate, and gentle. It was then that he willingly took up the name Daemon and became known only by that name to all but three people, his mother, his father, and Olivia. No one else used his given name, even in official functions it was not even mentioned, Vladimir was only a name he used when he signed official documents and orders.

Allowing the merger of three separate entities within himself was not without great cost, in doing so Daemon sacrificed a large part of who he was as a person, who Vladimir was as a person to become this new being. He also had to accept the wrongs and guilt of two whole other lives besides his own. The process, in which Vladimir became Daemon, almost drove him mad from the mental torment and anguish he faced when he allowed himself to be fully confronted by both Aodhan and his grandfather's essences. He had fought them off until he was ready to undertake what he knew was going to be the nearly insurmountable task of accepting the two essences that he had taken into himself.

His resistance of it alone had almost driven Vladimir mad, but to allow Aodhan and his grandfather to become one with him had drove Vladimir to the very brink of insanity. It had so very nearly driven him over that narrow precipice into the realm of insanity. That Daemon often wondered if he hadn't really gone insane after all, and when he had returned, he had returned as Daemon. He returned powerful and dangerous, with knowledge that no Immortal his age should have, carrying secrets that would curl the hairs on even Olivia's head.

Every time Daemon closed his eyes he saw everything *HE* had done, meaning everything he had done as Vladimir, everything he had done as Aodhan, everything he had done as Victor, his grandfather. He remembered every life that he had taken, ever dying scream he had ever heard, the expressions on the faces of every one of his victims. These things haunted him even in his waking hours, he would wake drenched in sweat, heart pounding, from a vivid dream in which he would replay the past over and over again in his head.

    A small part of him was calm and collected, viewing the images that played in his head without any pity, though he was remorseful for what he had done. This calculating, methodical, and heartless part of him allowed Daemon to get back to sleep quickly; this was the part of him that allowed Daemon to survive, to endure it all stoically. He had resigned himself to his fate long before he had allowed himself to become Daemon and knew there was no amount of repenting that would cleanse him of what he had done so he did not try for atonement.

    Instead he did his duty to his people as the Crown Prince and as the Regent, working like a man possessed to right the wrongs of his grandfather. To enforce the new laws of the land Daemon took drastic measures and made examples out of any criminal that he caught and found guilty. As the Master of the Knights of the Royal Guard he disbanded the need for a pedigree in the Academy so that all who wished to become Knights could if they survived the new training and curriculum that was enforced in the Academy. Daemon made inroads with many of the human rulers of the communities around his estate. Establishing trade and commerce with them, helping build the human villages into cities in which he had power and influence.

    At the end of these fifty years Daemon returned to Coelum to attend his mother's official coronation as Empress, his father, waited fifty years upon his mother's insistence to see if Daemon would take the throne, which she insisted was his rightful place once she learned what had really transpired the night Victor Daemon's grandfather had died. As tradition dictated, the Emperor had to wait two decades to declare a mistress as his mate and Empress. Daemon stayed at the palace as his father wished, but he was not comfortable with the lavishness of the lifestyle he held while in the palace.

    His estate was modest in regards to most Noble's estates. Being only three wings and three stories tall, and situated on a small plot of land, no more than a hundred acres. Small compared to the other lavish homes of the Immortal Nobles. The rest of the nine thousand acres of land Daemon was leasing out to human settlers and allowing them to build their towns and villages on the land, the same humans that he was making trade deals with and more were coming every day lured by the thought of good land and the wealth that the land could provide.

    Sitting in the study of his room at the palace there was a knock on his door and his mother entered. She hesitated at the threshold scenting the air. Daemon, looked at her and knew what it was that had caught her attention. His scent, it had changed from the one he'd had at his birth, when she had scented him after he had drunk from Aodhan it had been deeper and older than it should have been. This had confused her, then again at his ordaining his scent had changed because he had drunk from his grandfather, but then the scent had been too muddled by other scents to tell just how much it had changed.

Daemon rolled his head to the side and inhaled deeply, he knew his own scent by heart. Like an old forest of cedar and pine it was to him, though when he had been younger it had been young and fresh, less dangerous. To his mother the difference was clearly noticeable; his scent was clearly not just old anymore. It was ancient and foreboding, like the center of the Great Northern Woods that he had called home for the first part of his life. Only his scent was heavier, it enveloped the senses like a heavy blanket and if he wanted to it could be appealing or it could be a noxious fume. Daemon stood and bowed his head to his mother, his shoulders and arms relaxed.

He spoke first, breaking the nervous silence that had built in the short period of time it took for his mother to register the fact that his scent was much older and stronger than it should be.

"Mháthair tráthnóna maith cad a thugann tú le mo ndlísheomraí sin go déanach san oíche?" *Good evening mother, what brings you to my chambers this late in the night?* Daemon said lightly as he leaned against the desk easily. His mother looked startled and she answered hesitantly but not in kind. Speaking not in her native tongue but in the Ancient tongue of the Immortals. She gave him a more formal response.

"I was hoping that you would join your father and I for dinner, it has been a long time since either of us has seen you." She said slowly. Daemon bowed his head with a small smile and reached out for his mother's hand, noticing for the first time how delicate her hands were.

These hands had always dispensed such merciless justice when it was needed, even unto him when he deserved it as a cub, small and delicate but stronger than steel when needed. Daemon looked up at his mother and smiled again. He did not blame her for her apprehension of him. After all he had changed a great deal, but he was still her son.

"I would love to join you and father for dinner." He said lightly releasing his mother's hand.

She turned and he followed her out of the room after tying his sword to his belt and down the hall to the throne room where his father was waiting. His mother sat on his father's right hand side at the head of the table, and Daemon took the seat to his father's left. There were several other faces at the table; he recognized a few of them as the high Lords and ladies of the high noble court and their children. Olivia was there and she tried to catch Daemon's eye many times over the course of the meal, but Daemon refused to acknowledge her. At the end of the meal, Daemon excused himself and returned to his room where he recorded the events in his Compendium.

    On the days preceding and the day of his mother's coronation Daemon oversaw security proceedings himself, he knew his mother was not the most popular choice of Empress and there were many that would halt her accent to the throne if they could and many already had. If his mother had not been an adept warrior in her own right she would not be here at this moment, Daemon would have hated to see what would have happened if he would have had to revenge himself on his mother's murderers, or if his father got a hold of them. His father was no warrior but that did not make him incapable of killing.

He tripled the amount of security that had been originally been planned at the last minute and he himself led his mother's personal Guard. There was not one thing that he left out of place. He escorted his mother from her room to the adjoining room of the throne room where she would get ready for the coronation. Daemon remained with her through everything, one gauntleted hand on the hilt of his sword and his eyes looking about for assassins in the shadows. When his mother was ready and Kain had announced her, Daemon led her through the door and into the throne room. Up through the aisle of saluting Knights and to the dais on which his father stood waiting Daemon led her unfalteringly. The scene was similar to Daemon's coronation; to his father's left was a thin man in robes holding a cushion with a crown and signet ring.

Both symbols of the position his mother would hold. Daemon took his place on his father's right hand side and watched the crowd of Nobles for any sign that they would try to disrupt the ceremony. Though with the impressive show of force he had in the room he doubted it.

The ceremony was quick and went uninterrupted; his mother was crowned Empress of night and now sat on a throne beside his father as the Nobles celebrated halfheartedly around them. Daemon retreated to a corner of the room beside his parents and watched the unfolding festivities carefully. He was anxious because everything was progressing so smoothly, his instincts, all of them screamed at him that something was wrong. His eyes swept the throne room for any hint of the danger that he felt was approaching swiftly. He caught sight of it in the form of a Knight behaving oddly; the man was jumpy, and kept his sword drawn partway out of the sheath.

Daemon motioned four Knights to his side and approached the Knight. The man did not even wait for Daemon to reach him before drawing his sword and bellowing something in the guttural language of the Immortals about the Council of Ten and lunging at Daemon. Who dispatched the man with little effort and set his men to cleaning up the mess. He then turned to the room and hissed dangerously.

"I suggest any other would be assassins leave this party immediately or they will meet the same fate as this poor fellow." Daemon moved off to his parent's sides again, ignoring his parents looks of sheer pride. Daemon was more concerned with what the man had said before attacking him. He had annihilated the Council of Ten, obliterated them, and wiped them out of existence.

The Council of Ten should not still exist, unless a group of lesser Immortals took it upon themselves to reform the Council. But he could not do anything about that, they hadn't broken any laws as of yet. Shortly after his mother's coronation party ended Daemon returned to his estate. Both to investigate the instance if there was a new Council of Ten, and the implications that would have on his father's rule if they were allowed to gain any power.

Volume One

Book Two

Pack Beginnings

Volume One

Prelude

The moon was high and full. Hanging low in the night sky over the little farming village. It was the Festival of The Moon and the villagers were celebrating this Ancient festival with such a display of exuberance that the land around them felt lively and full of life. There was much dancing, feasting, and drinking as the celebration carried on into the night the moon raising onto a high peak in the starry sky. A young man dressed in the skin of a panther danced about the bonfire, teasing the younglings and wrestling with the older men as he strove to impress the many young ladies that danced provocatively by the fire.

There were several other young men who were dressed similarly to him in the skins of animals they had hunted and killed, but not one of them matched this young man's brawn. He was built like a mighty bull with a broad chest and narrow hips. His shoulders and arms were packed with muscle that flowed smoothly with his movements and knotted powerfully when he flexed them in irritation or to impress the young lasses that eyed him, his legs too were equally powerful. This man was the pride of the village, young Ayden McMann the strongest lad that worked the fields and the only lad brave enough to hunt in the Black Woods to the east of the village.

    Ayden was a modest man and cared only for looking after his family, of which he only had his siblings left. Six siblings he had to look after and a small farm that he had to keep running. His father had died of illness and his mother of grief shortly after, leaving him two elder sisters and four rowdy younger brothers to look after. In order to take care of his family and their homestead Ayden worked from the wee hours of morning until well after dark. His siblings woke early in the morning to help him, though never as early as he, if he could help it. His sisters were fine young ladies and they managed the house, while Ayden handle everything else nearly singlehandedly.

    His brothers did what they could for him in the fields. Even with all that they did for him,

Ayden still pulled most of the weight. After working the fields Ayden would hunt to put meat on their table and for the furs to supplement their income from the produce that they could sell. Ayden twirled around and around the bonfire thinking about home and his siblings as they danced by the great blaze, laughing merrily. It was rare that they got a chance to come into town to participate in these gatherings, but he was glad that they'd had the time to come this year. He was thinking it was about time that he begin to mediate match making sessions for his sisters and brothers.

    They were all getting to that age now, his sisters would come of age in a few weeks' time and they would want husbands of their own soon. He could see them making eyes at a few of the lads that were dancing around the fire with him. And his brothers would be men soon; they would need to find suitable wives of their own, as he had not. That would always be his most well kept secret. He fancied not the ladies, but should it come to be known where his fancies actually lay. The village would cast him out, possible even kill him for it.

Shaking himself from those morbid thoughts Ayden smiled at his brothers as they joined in the dance and festivities. He continued to whirl around the bonfire and sing along with his comrades letting his strong rolling voice rise and fall in the songs and hymns of the village. He may not be the oldest of his siblings, but he was undisputedly the master of the house.

When the moon began to fall Ayden began his journey home, alone. The moon shining off his pale blonde hair and mirth filled emerald green eyes as he waved off the other town's folk. He left his siblings with their respective partners for the night. These suitors would more than likely become their life partners. Ayden trusted his siblings to no end; he knew they would come home to him in the morning, probably with their partners in tow so that they could introduce them to him. The lane was dark and the going was slow as Ayden was very inebriated by the amount of ale he had imbibed at the celebration and the lane was muddy from the spring rains that had passed through the day before.

    He was not paying any attention to his surroundings as he sung a drunken tune to the wind as he stumbled along the lane. So Ayden did not notice the eyes that watched him from the shadows of the trees. He did not hear the soft padding of footsteps behind him in the grass. When the howling of a lone wolf started nearby it caught Ayden totally unaware but he was unafraid of just one wolf. He was a large man, and even inebriated he could take care of himself or so he thought.

    Ayden continued to walk along the lane towards his home. The howling grew closer and faded off, chilling him to the bone. He did not like how close the wolf sounded and now the dead silence that was building around him as he walked unnerved him greatly. The only sound that he could hear was his own labored breathing and the squelch of his boots through the mud of the lane. After the howling faded off, Ayden walked maybe another twenty feet before something large, strong, and ferocious ripped him off his feet and plowed him into a nearby tree beside the road before tumbling him in the grass.

Ayden did not know which way was up, all he knew was pain as teeth and claws ripped into him. Even in the moon light he could barely make out the things form. It was like a man from the shoulders down to its waist, with a broad chest and brawny arms ending in broad hands tipped with cruel claws. From the waist down it resembled a dog or wolf standing on its hind legs. Ayden could feel fur on his face and knew that the entire being was covered in it. Lashing out Ayden struck the things lupine head and made it recoil from him. Scrambling back to the road Ayden crawled through the mud feeling hot blood gush from his wounds.

The beast was on him again claws and fangs digging into his flesh as he screamed. The beast's eyes flashed green in the moon light and Ayden fought with every ounce of strength that he possessed splashing the road about him with blood and torn fabric. Covering himself in slick mud, making it harder for the beast to get a good hold on him. But it did, it's claws dug into his flesh and held him as still as it could. The beast found his throat and Ayden knew that would be the end of him, but still he roared his fury into the night and tore his hands on the beasts teeth trying to wrench the things jaws apart. Ayden was strong, perhaps the strongest lad in the village. But he was nothing compared to this beast's strength.

As the moon reached the western rim of the world Ayden was fading. He hung on to the sight of the full moon dipping below the trees far to the west were the village was, were his siblings were still out celebrating. Time seemed to freeze into place for Ayden preserving that one image in his mind. The full moon in all its glory and his last thought as darkness came to claim him was that it was the most beautiful sight he had ever seen. And how he wished he could have shared it with the people he loved. The moonlight shone down on a single tear that escaped Ayden's eye as they fluttered closed. Looking down on the young man the creature howled, not in victory but in misery.

***

Slowly the creature took the shape of a well-built man who was at least shorter than the injured young man by a head and a half, but would have been normal height otherwise. His eyes flashed green in the light as he looked over the lads still form assessing the damage that he had done. Ayden's throat was shredded, and his chest and stomach looked much the same, and he had lost a lot of blood. The man did not know if the lad would survive much longer, but he knew that the young man was alive for now, his sensitive ears could hear the faint beating of the lads strong heart.

The man lifted the young man easily and bore him away, he willed for this young man to survive. Because no ordinary man had the strength of will to continue fighting after he knows he is dead, and no ordinary man would weep at the sight of the full moon as if it was the most beautiful and precious thing they had ever seen. Running the man took off into the east with the lad he'd attacked, running full tilt for the forest that the village feared. The man reached the forest with Ayden around dawn and broke the camp he had made there. He dressed in his fine garments and wrapped Ayden in a rough blanket before slinging him over the withers of his horse and swinging himself into the saddle. Ayden's heart was beating frantically now, and his body was slick with sweat.

The man kicked his horse into a gallop and skillfully navigated through the trees. The forest ran on for many miles in either direction, but it was not very thick. Travel was relatively swift and easy through it. The rumors regarding it were only superstition, well founded superstition, but superstition nonetheless. The man pressed his horse to the limits of its endurance for many days before he came to a modest estate surrounded by a wall, topped with wolves in various poses. The main gate was made of wrought iron and it was opened by two Guards with eyes that flashed green in the dim light of the dying sun. The man entered and rode his horse right up to the heavy oaken doors of the manor house.

The doors opened and a tall obviously well-built young man stepped out, dressed simply in a white linen tunic and black leather breaches with a sword belted at his hip, his feet were enclosed in calf high leather boots that fit him well. His ebony hair hung down to his shoulders in waves and his face was shadowed by the stubble of a beard. Ebony eyes pierced the man as the young man's scent enveloped him, an Ancient pine and cedar forest. The man bowed his head and dismounted before pulling Ayden off the horse. The young man looked at the man coolly before saying.
"Lord Carmelito, I did not think you had it in you to actually hunt a human." The young man said turning to the side and motioning for the man to enter the grand house.

Carmelito sighed and made his way up the stairs and into the house. Holding the young man he'd attacked carefully. So as not to aggravate the wounds he'd caused further. "Thank you Lord Daemon, you have no idea how much this means to me." He said as he moved into the house, his eyes sweeping the foyer that he had entered. The young man, Lord Daemon smiled and led the way to a room where Carmelito could put his charge down to rest. Daemon opened a heavy door and snapped at a maid to bring hot water to prepare a bath. He watched as Carmelito placed his charge in the bed and covered him up. Daemon had an expression of curiosity on his face as he watched Carmelito.

"What prompted you to spare him Carmelito? Your father is King of the Southern Packs and their ways demand the life of a human before you can reach maturity in their eyes." Daemon said lightly looking at his nails. "You have failed twice already, if this one lives you will have failed three times and your life will be forfeit." Carmelito nodded and took the fevered young man's hand in his own.

"I could not kill him, he cried at the sight of the falling moon like it was the most beautiful and precious thing he had ever seen and he fought, this man fought bravely to the very end." Carmelito said softly, Daemon smiled and turned to leave the room.

"Lord Carmelito, you will always have a place in our Courts, my father and I will protect you from your father." Daemon said lightly as he left.

***

Ayden was drowning in fire; his entire body was seared in agony. But he could not move, he could not even scream. Fighting against the pain Ayden struggled, holding onto himself, memories of his past and of his family. For a while that helped ease the pain, but then nothing worked as the pain built to a peak and obliterated all thought, all other feeling. Ayden felt the pain keenly, but could do nothing to express or release it. The agony lasted for what seemed like an eternity before it finally began to fade from his body.

When the pain was finally and completely gone Ayden's breathing slowed and evened out. His eyes saw nothing because they were closed, but he heard everything, from the lightest flutter of a butterflies wing to the steady beating of what he thought was a drum. He could smell everything, wood, stone, leather, and a heady floral scent like roses and some other flower that he could not name. He identified this scent as his own as it seemed to be coming from him. There was another scent in the room, deep heady scent like freshly turned earth. There was a sound like rustling fabric and a cool voice spoke to him.

"Open your eyes cub, it is time to wake." The voice said softly. Ayden could not refuse that voice and opened his eyes. They flashed green in the dim candle light as he looked to the source of the voice. A man stood beside him, his hazel eyes viewing Ayden with pride and warmth. "Welcome my son, rise and dress yourself I have much to explain to you."

Volume One

Chapter One

Ayden looked around the room he was in and at the man that was beside his bed. The man who had spoken was standing right beside the bed and another man, who looked to be nearly as tall as Ayden was standing near the door he had just entered. The only sensible exit out of the room. Ayden paid close attention to the man beside the bedside. He was a very well built man, much like Ayden and the other man in the room, like they were used to hard labor, very hard labor. The man who had just entered the room had an appealing pine and cedar scent, which was strong and foreboding.

It invoked within Ayden an instinctive fear of the man. This other man. The one whom was beside the bed, the man who was looking down on Ayden with such warmth in his hazel eyes, reminded Ayden of a wolf, perhaps it was his fanged grin or the manner in which his words reverberated in his throat like a growl. But he reminded Ayden distinctly of a wolf. The man backed away from the bed as Ayden tossed the blankets off of himself. He was amazed at the sight, his clothes, or what was left of them were stiff, blood stained, and shredded, but there was not a mark on him, not one single scratch marred his flesh, nor scar marked his flawless tanned skin. Sliding out of the bed he stood towering over the man, confused he held his hands up before his eyes and flexed his fingers in disbelief.

    He could not believe that he was alive; the last thing he remembered was the sight of the beautiful full moon he had beheld and witnessed as he had lay dying in the lane thinking it would be the last thing he would ever witness in this life. He of course remembered brief flashes of the attack, the horrendous pain, it seemed false now in the light of this new day and his unmarked skin and the heavy breaths he was taking in as his anger began to rise in his confusion. Ayden remembered that, and that was all, he could not remember nothing else save for hazed fragments of agonizing pain and moments of conversation concerning him. But he only remembered generalizations, nothing else.

"Who are you? And why are you calling me your son?" Ayden asked when he could find the words to speak.

He was wary and on guard with the man, he did not know what to expect with these men let alone what they wanted with a poor farmer. This seemed to be a lavish room compared to his rather plain room back at the farm house. The man smiled again and bowed his head like he was carrying a great weight upon his broad shoulders.

"I am Carmelito, and I am your sire in this new life that you will be leading." The man said calmly. Ayden could not understand what Carmelito was saying, new life? Hadn't he just drunkenly imagined it all? He was not even injured, not even a scab or scar to show for what had happened so hadn't it all been a dream? "What do you mean new life? Where am I?" Ayden asked getting frustrated with the whole situation.

Carmelito held his hands out to the side to calm him and closed his eyes opening them again very slowly, they flashed green in candle light. Ayden fell back against the bed in shock. His heart hammering in his chest from fear. What were these people? What did they want with him? Ayden growled the low rumbling sound surprising him and making him stop and wonder what that was. Carmelito spoke softly and calmly, his tone relaxing Ayden despite Ayden's anxiety.

"You, my son are no longer human because I am not human, and I bit you nearly two months ago on the night of the full moon." Carmelito said gesturing to Ayden. "Since I bit you that night you have changed, you have turned into something more than human." Ayden shook his head angrily he could not accept what this man said as truth.

 This had to be an elaborate jest, though he did not know why such lordly men would choose him to pull this childish prank. He was just a simple farmer and he said as much.

"I am just a simple farmer, I can't be anything else, I do not know what game you are playing at but I'd like to take my leave of it now." Ayden said angrily his voice rough as he moved to push past Carmelito. "I have a family that I have to take care of." Carmelito stepped quickly into his path to the door and showed his teeth revealing again his fangs and how very real they were. Rage and fear boiled in the pit of Ayden's' stomach and burned in the heart of Ayden's chest, making heat wash down Ayden's spine along with a wave of agony and a sound similar to a panthers snarl rose from his throat in response to the challenge. Carmelito snarled in response. But not in anger, but like a father wolf would if their pup was misbehaving.

"You cannot go back to them, you can never go back to them, you are not human you are Immortal, a Lycanthrope." Carmelito growled at him warningly pushing him back towards the bed. He possessed more strength than Ayden would have believed the smaller man could have ever summoned up if he was human. If Ayden had not been so surprised by the action he would not have moved an inch. Instinctively he knew he was already much stronger than Carmelito.

Now that Carmelito had his full attention he growled out.

"Listen to me well cub, you are a Lycanthrope now, an Immortal and you are dangerous, far more dangerous than you could ever dare believe." Ayden snarled and pushed back instinctively lifting his lips over his teeth as the sound ripped the still air. He shuddered feeling suddenly very powerful, oh so very powerful, the feeling washed over him in waves, he could change, transform into something better, stronger and rip this puny man before him apart, and his instincts were screaming it at him. It was like something within him was coiling tight, a thread stretching taunt along his spine ready to break, a thread of confusion and rage. But when he looked at the other man in the room his blood ran cold with ice and he regained some measure of composure, if he were to lose control and reach out to kill Carmelito, that man leaning ever so casually against the door would surely kill him with no hesitation.
"I *AM HUMAN!*" he roared at them angrily trying to deny the truth, though he could see in both

their eyes that they could not be lying. Ayden had a gift of telling when a person lied to him.

Perhaps because he was a very good liar himself though he was a honest man at heart. But he knew when someone was trying to fool him with their words. Carmelito believed whole heartedly in what he was saying, and it struck Ayden like a blow to the gut the realization that Carmelito might very well be telling the truth. He remembered the legends of his village telling of wolf men who took on the shapes of animals on the night of the full moon to hunt those that wandered to far from their homes at night, and those that survived the attack became the beast men themselves and turned to prey on their own families. "I cannot be anything else; I have to be human…" Ayden whispered as he fell back feeling like the floor was coming up to swallow him whole. Carmelito caught and steadied him with a grunt.
"All will be well cub, I will show you everything from here on out." Carmelito said softly as he let Ayden down gently, Ayden's head was whirling

with the thought of never being able to see his siblings again.

He knew why he must not, if what Carmelito said was true then he, himself, would be a danger to them. There were several reasons that Carmelito had told Ayden he could never again see his mortal siblings. First and foremost Ayden was a danger to them, secondly this was an age of superstition and though secrecy was not the law it was wise to maintain some amount of secrecy. Ayden suddenly springing from the wilderness after two months and being presumed dead would bring about a lot of questions that were not easily answered, especially after the mess that had been left on the lane.

Carmelito took his time explaining things to Ayden, though they seemed pathetic now as he explained them to him. Daemon remained in the room by the door listening intently as Carmelito explained himself to Ayden.
"...In my country, the customs and rites of passage are different then they are for the Immortals of this land." Carmelito said slowly as

he paced in front of a seated Ayden who had been calmed down and given a seat in a study like room off the main room. "Here in the north there is a series of tests that a Lycanthrope cub must pass before they are declared an adult…" Carmelito paused so that Ayden could absorb what he was saying. Ayden's expression was like an open book though he tried very hard to hide it.

    Carmelito could tell that Ayden was plainly interested though it looked like he just wanted to run away more than anything else. Ayden nodded for Carmelito to continue with his story and wringing his hands Carmelito did so. "…In my country, our cubs do no such thing we are tasked with a hunt when we reach the age of three hundred…" he started slowly his voice slipping into a thick accent. "Our hunt is not the typical hunt, for my kin likes the taste of man flesh, my kin are the monsters of your human legend…" Carmelito stated slowly Ayden's face was pale and his eyes were dead.
"You were out that night hunting to become a man by your countries laws? And you picked

me?" Ayden demanded softly his voice hissing out in anger. Carmelito sighed and rushed into his explanation.

"...You were the ideal prey, tall, strong, and separated from your fellows, at least ideal by my people's standards..." Carmelito said softly he shrugged his shoulders and said. "But when I had you down and was ready to finish you off, you looked at the moon and the expression on your face was the most heart breaking thing I had ever witnessed, because it was so serene and at peace I could not carry out the deed." Carmelito went silent for a long time before sinking to a crouch before the door and looking up at Ayden.

"...Perhaps it would have been better to have let you die than suffer the fate that I have thrust upon you..." Carmelito said sadly, his voice low and thick. "But it is far too late to regret what has been done, now is the time to decide where we go from here, there is much to learn, and I have much to teach you or you can leave this place and go your own way and learn what you will on your own the choice is yours." Ayden looked down at Carmelito, he could see pain in the man's eyes, he could see the regret and sorrow the man held in himself for what he had done to Ayden.

It took Ayden a long time to decide what to do, and all the while the other man who Carmelito had yet to introduce was watching with a slightly bemused expression on his face. This man finally spoke, his voice was smooth and commanding but at the same time rumbling like thunder as the scent of pine and cedar washed over Ayden, reminding him of an old dark forest. The scent gave him the chills, but the man's black eyes pierced him and held him as he spoke.

"What will it be cub? Will you stay? Or will you go? Make your choice now." The man commanded slowly, every word he spoke was a challenge and a command making Ayden want to respond, to immediately obey, as well as cower before the man or flee. Ayden looked to Carmelito and sighed making his choice.

"I will stay and learn, it doesn't seem like I have much of a choice otherwise." Ayden said after a great length. Carmelito stood and the dark eyed man by the door came forward. His silky voice speaking out again striking Ayden's ears like lightning.

"I am Lord Daemon, and I will be helping with your education as your sire has asked of me." The man said lightly running a hand through his wavy shoulder length hair. "But I must remind you both that I have other duties that I have to attend to so I will have a limited time to teach." Ayden nodded and stood as Carmelito bowed to Daemon. Lord Daemon left the room and Carmelito followed soon after leaving Ayden alone with his thoughts. He looked out the window as the sun rose tinting the sky outside the windowpanes a light pinkish gold. It was a beautiful day to start his new life. Perhaps there could be some good that came of this. With a sigh Ayden shook his head. Only time would tell. And he now had all the time in the world to figure things out.

Chapter Two

The first ten years of Ayden's Immortal life was spent learning everything his sire Carmelito and Lord Daemon knew about the Lycanthrope races, about what he himself was. As Ayden did not take the traditional shape of a wolf when he first shifted, a most painful experience that had caught Ayden off guard during a duel with Lord Daemon. Ayden took the form of a black panther, a majestic beast from the unexplored southern jungles of Hoarodvan, the nation to the south of Athartha. Carmelito explained to Ayden that the shape that he took and the color of his fur reflected who he really was as a person; Carmelito could only give Ayden the generals of his kind as he had not interacted with Ayden's lycan breed before though personally knowing them to be rather rare as were all the races of large were-cats.

Ayden learned quite a bit about his kind from Daemon whom had dealings with several were-cats of various breeds both large and small. The smaller breeds of were-cats were more common, and the larger breeds were rarer and most highly prized for their loyalty and ferocity in battle, lion's and panthers in particular. Also in those ten years under Carmelito's and Daemon's tutelage Ayden was put through the most brutal work that he had ever faced before. He thought working in the fields as a mortal was bad, Daemon had him lifting and hauling huge slabs of stone for miles. Dragging sleighs weighted down with chests upon chests of iron and lead through rough terrains no matter the weather. Training for hour's day in and day out to master his body and the way of the warrior. On the rare occasion that Ayden actually talked to Daemon, Daemon drilled into Ayden the need to follow the Emperor's laws.

  As Carmelito was seeking to renounce all ties with his father the King of the Southern Lands, and establish a life as a citizen in the Empire. It was imperative that the Emperor's laws be followed. They were simple, do not kill any mortal needlessly, do not commit an act of theft against another Immortal, and do not commit an act of murder against another Immortal amongst other more basic laws.

When these ten years came to an end Carmelito and Daemon took Ayden to a celebration of a Northern Pride, here Ayden participated in the trial of cubs. Carmelito watched with pride as his son took each trial in stride and surpassed each other cub in the pack, earning the ceremonial Tattoo's with distinction. Though the pride was very secretive about their trials, and Ayden refused to discuss the details of exactly went on during the events in question. Ayden came out of his Trials of the Cubs a changed man. There had been nine trials that the cubs faced in this pride, and there was only ever one survivor at the end.

The first trial was the Trial of Pain, the cubs were taken to a cave not far from the village and subjected to numerous tortures until they reached their utmost level of pain tolerance and eventually broke. This was done to remind them they were not invincible. Ayden absolutely refused to make a sound even till the last. He would not succumb to pain. For this the pride would tattoo him with a distinguished pattern on his forearms should he survive till the end of the trials. The next trial was the Trial of Stealth, for this they were unleashed into an underground obstacle course full of traps and trapped floorboards rigged to squeak should they step just right. Ayden was a creature of the woods and the night. The darkness was his ally and he took to the highest places and avoided the floor completely his keen eyes seeking a way out of the maze as his instincts guided him to the highest possible places naturally. He was the first one out of the maze and the first one to line up for the Trial of Speed.

When the rest of the cubs had lined up and the Task Masters sounded the start Ayden was off sprinting through the woods. Unlike with the wolves, the prides made full use of their abilities during each trial. And Ayden certainly made full use of every ability he had. Shifting his shape and allowing his instincts to guide him through the tangle of thick trees. His black form rebounding from tree to tree like a giant black arrow, he was fast but not the fastest of the group, but he was the best tactician in the group and used the terrain to his advantage allowing him to come in close to first, but that would not matter in the end. The Trial of Strength was the next trial the cubs had to endure.

It was actually a set of tasks to which they were set to, lifting impossible weights of iron, dragging immense caskets filled with lead, and climbing tall cliffs while weighted with lead chains. Ayden passed this challenge without flinching or turning away. He refused to back down. The next trial to test him was the Trial of Freedom. The cubs were each bound and locked down tight and told to escape, for some who were domestic felines this was easy they simply had to shift their shape to be free of their chains, but then there was getting free of the new maze, a bracken maze deep within the forest deep within the night. Ayden calmed himself and braced himself for the pain that he knew was to come, for to get out of the shackles that bound him he was going to have to dislocate his own wrist.

He could not risk breaking the shackles for fear of the sound of shattering metal attracting enemies to him. Not all the cubs were friendly to his presence in the trials. Though for now the trials forbade the cubs from killing each other, the Task Masters could easily turn a blind eye to an 'accident' here in the maze. Ayden growled as he wrenched his wrist out of place and slid the manacle off freeing one hand before popping the joint back into place quickly and moving on from that area, doing the same to the other wrist as he went to free himself completely so he could shift and get out of the maze.

Ayden went on to complete the Trial of Endurance, a trial where the cubs were placed in a sweltering environment meant to make them weak and exhausted, to make their hands slip. And they were to hold light weights, no more than a few pounds for as long as possible. The weights were slick in Ayden's hands as they were made of smoothed iron, and his sweat dripped from him. But he held onto them the longest even though he was all but fainting from the heat and sweating rivulets. It took the Task

Master prying the weights from his fevered hands when he had passed out for the trial to end. The Trial of Courage was something Ayden would not have minded telling his father about, as it was an exhilarating challenge, this trial challenged each of the cubs to launch themselves from the Fatal Cliffs, a plummet of nearly a thousand feet into frigid aconite poisoned waters.

    The water was so laden with aconite petals any given time of the year that it was nearly fatal to any immortal that ingested or bathed in the waters at the base of the falls or from the waters that flowed from it. It was similar to another smaller water fall in the Great Northern Woods, close to the Lady of the Woods village, Ayden had heard. Ayden was apprehensive about diving off the cliff into water that he knew was poison to him, Carmelito and Daemon had both warned him about the dangers of aconite. The flower it's self was dangerous to Immortals, but when it was properly prepared it became a deadly poison, or if the petals mixed with water and fermented that to could become a deadly poison to an Immortal, particularly Lycanthropes.

He looked over the edge of the waterfall and he could see literally thousands of blue petals covering the surface of the water save for where the waterfall foamed. Loch Na Bláthanna. *Lake of Flowers.* That was what this place was called and this fall, was called Titim nimh. *Poisoned Fall.* Fitting name for the place really. Ayden looked at the rest of the anxious faces around him and at the Task Master whom eyed him warily. Ayden stripped out of his tunic then his breeches before turning to the other cubs. "Tis but a dip in a pool of flowers." He said, let them ruminate on that he thought as he stepped backwards off the cliff and fell through the air.

He did not know how to swim but he figured he would learn quick enough. The shock of his body slamming into the water startled the air from his lungs and he swallowed water and a mouthful of petals. Frantically he paddled for the surface just as the undercurrent of the waterfall caught him and pulled him back under. Eventually Ayden got himself to the surface and to the bank of the lake where he heaved his guts out before collapsing by a patch of the evil blue flowers, none of the rest of the cubs jumped into the water. Ayden would be the only one advancing onto the rest of the trial if he survived the taint of the Aconite he had ingested.

The trial of Loyalty was much like the Trial of Pain only there was a point to the torture. A question, where does your loyalty lie? Ayden had determined that his loyalty was to Daemon above all else, Daemon was his Alpha. By all rights it should have been his father. But Ayden could not place his loyalty in a man who had abandoned his country without trying to change it, and Daemon, Daemon was an Alpha, his father was not. But he did not give this information away. Stubbornly he kept this information to himself, he refused to give in no matter what was done to him. In the end he was not broken and was released into the wilds to complete the next trial. The Trial of Survival, the other cubs were released into the wilds after him on their own trial, theirs was a Trial of

Redemption, and if they succeeded then they could try again at the Trial of the Cubs.

Their task, hunt and kill Ayden son of Carmelito, Ayden's task was to survive at whatever the cost and he did. When he returned back to the village nearly a year later, a changed man, but very much alive. He was marked with the tattoos of the elite champion, a feline who has excelled in every task, his entire body was covered from ankles to throat, save for the very sensitive areas. But when his father asked him what had really transpired during the events in question Ayden brushed him off and refused to answer. It was not out of spite, Ayden knew if he revealed to Carmelito what had transpired during his trials. The soft hearted man would have been devastated.

At the end of the trials Ayden watched the pride as they danced and celebrated much in a manner that his village had in the festival of the moon. The night he had been attacked by Carmelito. Daemon was separated from the festivities as he talked in depth with the Alpha of a visiting pack. She had brought a few of her pack mates whom were domestic were-cats for the trials. The visiting Alpha was a wild looking woman with ebony hair and a commanding presence. Ayden watched them as they spoke to each other, they seemed very absorbed in their conversation. Carmelito stayed with Ayden as he observed the pride at play. They did not talk, though they had grown close in the ten years that they had known each other. They just sat and enjoyed each other's silent company.

    Ayden had come to see Carmelito as a father figure in his life as hard as it had been to accept in the beginning that he was indeed an Immortal; Carmelito had been there whenever he needed him, no matter what he needed him for. Ayden thought to himself as he watched the festivities. If it had been ten years before this moment, he would have jumped in and celebrated with these people regardless of who they were. But now he was wary of them all, even the children.

    In those first ten years with his sire and Daemon Ayden had learned a very important lesson. Compassion and kindness were ill afforded weaknesses in this world where your enemies lurked around every corner, so Ayden learned to disguise his kindness and compassion. He learned to put up a mask. A mask that he modeled not after Carmelito, but after Daemon whom though he had little contact with. He admired Daemon's great strength and discipline and strove to make himself like that in every aspect of his life. Hardening his heart Ayden built his mask. But he did not lose himself to it. Daemon had tersely explained that would lead to his downfall. Never forget who you are. Daemon had said to him before the trials.

Daemon returned to them as the moon drew low in the western sky, and led them away from the festivities to their horses to undertake the long journey back to Daemon's manor. Ayden breathed in the cool night air and mounted his horse. The beast nickered and started forward at a nudge of Ayden's heels following in line after Carmelito and Daemon. Ayden would have preferred to run in his panther form, but two wolves and a great cat traveling together would cause some talk with the superstitious humans along the way. Three exceptionally well dressed men traveling together, no one would bat an eye at.

It took them a few months of hard riding to reach Daemon's estate, and through it all Daemon never let up on drilling Ayden about the laws, the structure of the Emperors Courts and Ayden's role in them. Carmelito kept quiet on these matters, because the lessons were just as much for him as they were for Ayden. When they reached the estate there was a carriage waiting for them, it was already loaded and the driver was waiting patiently for them. Ayden had barely stumbled off his horse before his father and Daemon were escorting him to the carriage and pushing him inside it. Daemon was the only one who spoke to Ayden as Carmelito was discussing with the driver the arrangements for the trip. "Your father is sending you to the Academy, but only because I have forced him into it." Daemon said coldly to Ayden as Ayden slumped exhaustedly in his seat. "There you will be given a formal education in the ways of the Empire and be inducted into the Knights of the Royal

Guard at the end of twenty four years if you survive the Academy." Daemon continued without even flinching, there was no remorse in his eyes.

Even after watching Daemon for a while. Ayden could not detect an ounce of sympathy either. There was no hesitation in Daemon's eyes when he had informed Ayden that he was sending him to a place where he could very likely die. Where Ayden would be expected to either survive or die. Daemon smiled wickedly at him and said coolly.
"Life or death, I wonder which path your feet will tread?" he closed the carriage door and Ayden felt his anger rise, he knew that Daemon was baiting him into a challenge. A challenge that could very well get him killed. Carmelito had briefly explained what Daemon was to him, who Daemon was, and what Daemon had to do to survive when he was younger, though Carmelito was not entirely sure on the exact details of what had actually occurred. As he himself had only been an emissary in the north for the

Volume One

period of time when Daemon had been at the Academy and with the Knights.

Ayden had heard the rumors that surrounded Daemon, and he had no doubt that Daemon was more than vicious enough to have done more than a few of the things the rumors said he did. Then there was the fact that Daemon remorselessly owned up to several of the rumors being fact. Knowing that Daemon was brutally honest did nothing to quell Ayden's trepidation. He would leave this place, and if he ever returned to his father. Ayden would be returning a changed man. The carriage started away and Ayden was rocked back into his seat.

The journey to the huge metropolis of the Immortals took around three months to complete, as the horses were sturdy and pressed to their limits each day. The richness of the capital city of the immortals, this city, Coelum, astounded Ayden. When he had first looked out the carriage window his eyes had nearly popped out of his head. He was awed by its sheer size, built right into the mountains it seemed to be. The carriage brought Ayden right up to a pair of massive iron gates that were closed to him. A diminutive man stood at the fore of them with a whip at his left hip and a short broad bladed sword on his right held up by a thick leather belt. He wore a breast plate, plated boots, bracers, and his head was capped by a decorated open faced helm. Ayden stepped out of the carriage and towered over this man who was half his size. But he did not make any move to push the man out of his way or to make this man subservient to him.

    He could sense the power that this little man held, his scent was strong and like Daemon's it reeked of age, though it was not quite as poignant as Daemon's who's scent was rich and powerful in its own right, intoxicatingly so. Ayden bowed his head to this man and said. "My name is Ayden, son of Prince Carmelito a high noble under the care of Lord Daemon the Regent." Ayden paused as the smaller man looked him over and motioned for him to continue. "I have come to claim a formal education so that I may join the ranks of the Knights of the Royal Guard." Ayden finished baring his fangs. The man walked tight circles around him and came back to the gate with a pleased look on his face.

"A farmer I am guessing, isn't that right boy? You probably haven't even seen real battle beyond the Trial of the Cubs, let alone held a sword for more than show before." The man stated with a smirk, Ayden felt his lip curling over his fangs in response. He wanted to refute the little mans claim. Daemon had trained him with a sword, Ayden had spent every waking moment he was not learning laws, or the Immortal language or hauling iron or stone perfecting the art of the blade, of wielding the blade in unison of his claws and fangs.

It was a unique skill for any lycan, and one that Daemon had perfected. Daemon had taught it to Ayden, and the man had not been merciful about it. Ayden had never thought of their sparring as anything less than a real battle. To have done so would have made Daemon furious and Ayden would not currently be here. It was not a common style for Immortals to use, most Lycanthropes found it too bothersome to hold a sword when shifted into their half form, though they could if they had the presence of mind to do so. Ayden did not just have the presence of mind to keep hold of his sword, but the discipline to use it as an additional weapon along with his natural weapons that he had gained when he had turned.

    He did not like this small man telling him that he would be less than useless with a blade. But he bore with it silently; the only evidence of his rising ire was the knotting of his thick brows and jaw muscles. It was true that he had yet to see real battle, but his sparing sessions with Daemon had been bloody and brutal and very, very real. Daemon had not been kind to him, had not shown him an ounce of mercy other than to spare him his life.

"I tell you now lad, this place is not for the week of body, the frail of mind, or the faint of heart." The man said with a wicked smile his hands resting on the gates of the Academy. Ayden realized that the smaller man was trying to get a rise out of him. "You will either die here or you will become a Knight of the Royal Guard, there is no quitting Lord Daemon made sure of that." Ayden fixed the man with a deadly glare and growled with utter certainty of his words.

"I will never quit, and I will not be so easily killed." The man chuckled and pushed the gates open and led Ayden inside.

Inside the Academy walls was marvelous, there were perhaps a dozen low buildings surrounding a large cobbled courtyard dominated by a raised stone dais at the far end by the largest of the low buildings. The man lead Ayden to a building to the far left, it was long, low and very broad. There was a single heavy iron door fitted into the wall of the building with only a single lantern beside it. The man walked Ayden right through the door and into the building. He led Ayden to a bunk just inside the door and pointed at it.

"Here be where you'll rest your head farmer boy, you can call me Commander Chase." The man said lightly as he turned to leave the hall with a smile. Leaving Ayden to view the hall with an appraising look and what he saw impressed him.

Row upon row of bunks stood with hardly room enough for a person of Ayden's size to maneuver about. Standing four bunks high and securely bolted to the ceiling and floor, there was enough room for an average sized man to sit up between each of the bunks but no other room could be garnered. And every bunk with the exception of the one that had been left for Ayden was filled. At the end of each of the bunks was a chest, Ayden sat on the edge of his bunk and unpacked his bags into his trunk, noticing the few belongings he had were few and sparse compared to the some of the cadets that wandered about the hall in fine clothes and jewelry. As he unpacked his belongings he uncovered a long cross shaped object wrapped in fine cloth.

Slowly Ayden began to uncover the object, revealing a smooth leather scabbard pitch black in color caped in gold, all the way up to a gold crosspiece and leather wrapped hilt, and a gold pommel shaped like a roaring panther's head. Reverently Ayden drew the blade from the sheath admiring the pattern on the blade, he had seen Daemon's blade up close a few times before, close enough to see the wolves running free through the knotted forest along the center fold of the blade. Ayden's blade was similar only instead of wolves there were panthers prowling through knots of vines along the blade. It was a thing of devastating beauty, but when he tested the edge he found it to be true and knew the blade to be a durable weapon of battle.

It was a bit of an older fashioned sword than the thinner and lighter rapiers that most of the richer cadets wore. Though their weapons were surely just as deadly as his monster of a blade. But this sword was the same shape and consistency of the blades Ayden had been trained with, if he wielded a smaller blade he would surely shatter it upon the first blow. The problem Ayden foresaw was whether or not any of the other cadets could wield their weapons as effectively as he could his own. Ayden did not dare to underestimate any of these cadets; those that were wearing their weapons wore them with familiarity. And from what his father had taught him of most Lycanthropes, they taught their young to use weapons, though the proud people usually frowned on using such methods preferring to use claw and fang to settle a dispute.

    Ayden unwrapped the belt from around the sheath and belted the sword around his waist letting it's weight settle around his hips comfortably. A farm boy he had been called, a farm boy he had once been, but no longer. He was an Immortal in every devastating meaning of the word. He barred his fangs and let out a wicked snarl as his hand fell to the pommel of the sword. Instinctively he knew who had given him the sword. There was only one person who would give him something like this and expect him to use it to further his position, Daemon. The man who had drilled into him the importance of rank and station when it came to the Immortal society, the one man who had challenged him to be something more than just average at every turn.

    This was going to be an eventful twenty four years, Ayden thought to himself. He unstrapped the sword from the belt noticing the belt buckle was that of a snarling panther head and smiled as he laid the sword by the head of his bed. And lay down to sleep knowing he would need the rest for the coming day.

Volume One

Chapter Three

The following morning found Ayden already up, alert, and completing a series of exercises to calm his nerves. Preparing himself for the day's trials that were sure to come. He belted on his sword at the first sound of the horn and headed for the door along with a string of the other cadets, a number of the others remained behind, either still sleeping or still rushing to get ready for the day. Ayden remembered the whip on Commander Chase's belt and knew the fate that waited those that were tardy would not be pleasant. He marched straight to the cobbled courtyard where he saw Commander Chase standing upon the dais and took a ready position before him, the other cadets gradually filled out behind him in a ragtag platoon. Only Ayden stood at attention and was silent as the horn faded into silence.

At Commander Chase's side were three men, a thin wiry man who held the Royal banner. Ayden recognized it as such because it also hung behind Daemon's chair in the main hall of his estate, and two heavily armored men who stood at attention beside him. When the final ringing call of the horn had faded into silence and the rest of the cadets had straggled out of the barracks into formation. Commander Chase began to speak what was obviously a well-rehearsed speech, one that had probably fallen on the years of thousands of young cadets ears before theirs.

"Listen well you filthy mongrels, here in this place I am your master, you will obey any order that I give you without question." Commander Chase stated in a slow growl, "Here in these halls you serve me." This was met with snarls of discontent and roars of outrage. Mostly from those dressed in finery and bearing the thin, jewel encrusted weapons, Vampires from the smell of them.

"You are a Lycanthrope, how dare you presume that we serve you! Your kind is not fit to even lick our boots." One haughty young Vampire snarled at the Commander.

Ayden rolled his head on his shoulders and put a hand on his sword as the Vampire opened his mouth to speak again. His father had warned him that this was the outlook that many of the Vampire Nobles had, and it irritated him to no end. The young Vampire was right beside him and blathering on and on about how the Vampire race was far superior to the lycanthropic race. As the impertinent youth continued on with his hateful dithering, the Commander was simply watching with a small smile. As if daring the youth to step forward and do something about it. Ayden could not take it any longer, one of the primary lessons that Daemon had instilled into him, was that in the Immortal society everyone rises and falls on their own power and determination to succeed. With a flash he drew his sword and was cutting down the blathering youth, he needed to make an example of the youth to get his point across.

    As the blood dripped down his face and blade Ayden snarled baring his fangs.
"Here we are all equal, we all bleed the same color, and we all have the same choices before us, life or death." Ayden said softly his voice echoing across the courtyard. "Every man and

woman here will rise or fall based on their desire to succeed and survive their desire to rise above the rest and exceed all expectation." Ayden wiped his blade on the dead man's tunic and sheathed his sword before looking up at the Commander to see an impressed expression on his face. He had repeated back to the Commander more or less the same words the man had spoken to Daemon a little over a century ago and had effectively silenced all those around him. Ayden smiled and snapped back to attention as Commander Chase lifted his head proudly, a stern expression on his face.

"I could not have said it any better myself Cadet Ayden, but that will be ten lashes for speaking out of turn and another twenty for taking a life without command, and the rest of you louts who were late will get twenty lashes at the post for your tardiness!" Commander Chase barked loudly his voice booming over the courtyard, Ayden hardly flinched at his pronounced punishment.

    Daemon had done much worse to him before than lashing him with a whip. Ayden regretted nothing of what he'd just done. He smirked as he was led first to the post, a large cross that had been erected to the far end of the courtyard sometime in the night, he could smell the freshness of the sawn wood. The two armored eunuchs pulled Ayden's arms out wide and clapped his wrists into irons drawing the chains tight over the wood cross beam of the cross and securing them with a heavy bolt. Commander Chase clapped Ayden on the shoulder before pacing out to the maximum extent of his whip. One of the eunuchs shoved a leather bit into Ayden's mouth and chuckled as they walked away and Commander Chase cracked his whip against the ground.

    Wincing as he straightened from the post Ayden rubbed his wrists. His tunic hung from him in bloody tatters and he moved away tearing the rest of the fabric from him so that the next in line could have their turn. The wounds on his back burned like he had been seared repeatedly with a hot iron. But this pain he could live with, now the cold seeping pain of feeling your life slipping away because your sparring partner had mercilessly ripped you open till you were near gutted like a fish, now that pain he did not want to feel again. Ayden stalked to the sidelines and watched as another twenty cadets received their punishments.

He used the shredded linen strips of his tunic to bind the wounds on his wrists, when the disciplinary show was over the rest of the cadets lined back up, Ayden somewhere in the middle. Commander Chase cocked his head to the side and looked at the sun, which was high now.
"Now that we have that over with, each and every one of you is going to gear up, and you see that little stone over yonder? You are going to lift and carry it for a little hike through the mountains." Commander Chase pointed over to a massive stone which Ayden had mistaken for a building the night before. Ayden felt his eyebrows rise a bit at the task laid before them. He nodded his head and led the rush to the garrison to grab their gear.

Inspecting the stone Ayden found that there were steel rods placed evenly across the bottom of the stone maybe a hundred or more. He seized a rod and waited, the other cadets took their places and they all strained to lift the stone. Ayden growled and brought the rod just below his chest. Commander Chase snapped his whip and shouted from his dais.

"One hundred miles you mongrels hurry it up or you will not be eating tonight." Ayden was the first to take the very first step forward and continued to set the pace over the mountainous terrain as the sun began its descent into the west. The weight of the stone was crushing, constantly bearing down on the group as they marched determinedly. It did not take more than a few hours for Ayden to put himself in a position of leadership within the group, though a few heads came flying free of their shoulders for him to take that position. With the fight for the leadership position settled and dusk coming on swiftly Ayden set a harsh pace through the rocky terrain, tempers were high, but Ayden kept them in line and working together long after the premature night had fallen and well after the first stars were out.

Leading them with his superior senses alone, that was not to say that he did not make mistakes. Ayden made plenty that cost them precious time and daylight. When Ayden finally called the halt and had them start up camp, every single one of them were exhausted, even Ayden who was well used to this by now thanks to Daemon's harsh training. Many of these Immortals though were pampered Nobles, or the newly turned looking to make a name for themselves. Very few were accustomed to hard work either in the present or previous life. Ayden set up his tent a little away from the main camp and shifted his shape fully. Slipping into the shadows of the night he left to scout the areas around them, and see if he could find a safe path back to the Academy. This was as much for him as it was for the rest of the Immortals in his platoon. After all it would not be much fun if it was just him after he found his way back to the Academy.

Ayden scoured the mountains for the remainder of the night memorizing them and the paths that would lead him and the platoon safely back to the Academy. He returned to his tent a few hours before dawn and brought it down swiftly and quietly before waking his comrades and setting them to work dismantling the camp site and preparing the stone for their departure. Tempers were already soaring high as the rest of the platoon took their positions with groans and grunts. Everyone was hungry, cold, and sore from the previous days march. Ayden was dead tired but he was determined not to give in, Daemon had put him through worse. This was nothing compared to what Daemon had done. This was heaven compared to that. Ayden bent down to grab the rod that had been sunk into the side of the stone the day before only to realize that it was gone, the only thing that was in its place was a hole four inches in diameter, and threaded like a screw.

    Ayden stood up and looked around and smiled baring his fangs looking at the mountains around them. This was his fault, he hadn't set a watch, and he hadn't felt the need to. They were after all not in enemy territory. A fool he was to think that of all things. Ayden slipped his pack off his shoulders and dug around until he found the rope that had been bundled into the bottom. There was at least fifty feat of the finest silk rope in the world in each of these packs. Ayden thought quickly looking about him, the area was indeed mountainous and there were a few sparse trees growing here and there, they would be of no use. Digging through his pack some more Ayden found ten long heavy steal spikes and a hefty hammer. An idea struck him then, there were perhaps two hundred Immortals in the platoon, if he put the strongest up front pulling on the ropes and the rest pushing from behind then they could get this monolith of stone back to the Academy relatively safely.

    He stood and began barking orders, quickly separating the strongest of the platoon from the others and beginning the preparations on the stone again to get it underway. Ayden himself stood at the fore of the pack at the front of the stone, he knew it was another fifty miles to the Academy and he was determined to make it by nightfall. The spikes had been driven into the stone at an angle and the ropes tied securely to them, and each rope was held by one or more Immortals. At the back of the stone the remaining hundred and fifty cadets waited the command to push. Ayden knotted the rope around his hands and snarled he looked around him and nodded before bellowing the command to go forward and lurching against the rope. Around him fifty other cadets did the same and the stone lurched forward a few feet and began a slow grating slide forward over the rocky ground. Ayden set the pace, taking great lunging strides with every step.

  They continued on into the night and Ayden led them true with every step, even though he was all but falling down with exhaustion, Ayden continued to lead them straight up to the Academy gates and through them. He dropped his rope and climbed to the top of the stone and heaved his spike free of the stone, recoiling his rope as he walked back to drop down. Commander Chase was walking towards them with an astonished smile on his face.

"I'll have to say you are a remarkable farm boy Ayden son of Carmelito." Commander Chase said lightly as Ayden stopped before him.

The man looked Ayden over and then over at the rest of the cadets. Like he was counting heads, and he did not look surprised to see that several were missing from the ranks.

"I see that you are the Commander, you sure you can handle the position farm boy?" Commander Chase asked lightly. Ayden bared his fangs letting them gleam in the moonlight and roared in response, letting the sound of it echo across the mountains. When the ringing of his roar faded to a dull echo he looked back at the now bemused Commander Chase.

"I have never been more ready." Ayden said slowly as he glared down at the man. Commander Chase smiled in response and patted his whip.

"That means that whatever they do while under your command, falls back on you, so you better be clear with them, very clear what it means to cross you." Commander Chase said softly leaning in with a slight wink. He called out to the rest of the cadets.

"There is food in the feeding hall, lights out in thirty." The Commander stated coldly before marching away. Ayden organized the remaining cadets and led them to the feeding hall. He himself ate halfheartedly before leading the way back to the barracks to find his bunk to sleep.

Chapter Four

    Ten years passed for Ayden. He grew into a fearsome leader, he did not quite gain the renown and fame that his idol Daemon had possessed while he had been at the Academy. But Ayden did have a measure of renown and fame that could be compared to Daemon's when Daemon had been younger. Ayden had proved to be an exceptional student and leader, much like Daemon had. He proved to be a calculating man with a ruthless demeanor. There was no one that he allowed to stand in his way, or question his orders. Ayden did not achieve as high of a cadet ranking as Daemon had, but he came close, very close. The only reason he did not succeed in achieving a higher ranking than platoon Commander was the fact that he challenged the status quo.

    He questioned the authority and intelligence of his instructors, and if he found them inferior to himself, he killed them. Not once however did he challenge Commander Chase, he could smell the age in the small man's veins and knew from the ease in which the man carried himself that he was a seasoned warrior, also he respected the small man greatly.

    Ayden woke his fellow remaining cadets well before the sounding of the first horn to dress them in their full gear and prepare them for the coming inspection. They would be inspected by their new Commander as well as Commander Chase to ensure they had received the best training and education that the Academy offered before becoming soldiers in the Emperors army. Ayden ran his hands through his hair and across the ceremonial sash that bore all his medals of achievement. He had a feeling that this was going to be an ominous day. Growling he readied his men and waited for the sound of the summoning horn as he inspected them endlessly. Perfecting perfection as Commander Chase would have called it. When the sound of the summoning horn came Ayden led his cadets out and into the courtyard and formed them up.

    They stood at attention ready for whatever order they would be given. Ayden looked them over, surveyed the men on the dais, noting that Commander Chase was absent for the time being he put his platoon at rest. They waited patiently as the sun came up over the eastern mountains for the Commander to appear. It was only when the sun was fully formed and they were beginning to bake in their armor that the Commander appeared and he was not alone. Beside him was a tall handsome figure, dressed in the heavy armor of a Knight, though this armor was hardly standard issue as it was patterned with wolves and forests. Under one arm was the man's helmet and it was molded in the likeness of a snarling wolfs head, and the gap in the animals snarling maw served as the eye slits. Ayden instantly recognized this man as Daemon, he did not have to scent the pine and cedar scent that seemed older than time to know that face.

Ayden snapped to attention and his cadets did likewise as the Commander and Daemon approached. Ayden drew his sword and saluted crying in unison with his platoon.

"Hail Crown Prince Daemon!" Daemon stopped before Ayden and nodded his head with a pleased smile. He turned to Commander Chase and said.

"These are some fine soldiers you have trained Commander, do you mind if I have a word with their platoon Commander for a moment? He and I have much to discuss before we depart." Commander Chase bowed his head and responded lightly with a small smile.

"No my Lord, they are under your command from here on out, what you do with your men is your will not mine." Commander Chase then took his leave with a low bow and Ayden met Daemon's eyes with a fiercely proud look. Daemon motioned with his head and stepped away. Ayden put his platoon back at rest and followed after him, catching up to him quickly.

    They seemed to wander aimlessly through the Academy grounds for a while in silence. Daemon broke that silence only after they had reached the stables.

"I have heard many great things about you since you entered the Academy, it is good that you have proved yourself capable and quick to learn." Daemon said lightly as they came to a stop before the stable entryway. "It is good because I have no use for imbeciles under my command, particularly those that are my commanding officers." Ayden felt his jaw slacken in shock of Daemon's words.

    But he was quick to recover and act unperturbed by Daemon's statement. He however did want to know how this was going to affect him, and just how much responsibility Daemon was placing upon him.
"What does that mean Lord Daemon?" He asked quickly, Daemon smiled and produced a Knights Commander medal from his belt pouch. It was unlike any traditional Knight Commander medallion that Ayden had ever seen, instead of the typical dragon's head that was under the crossed swords underneath the olive laurels, there was a panthers head and the medal was made of gold, not silver. Daemon offered it to him and he took the weighty medal with reverence.

"It would mean Lord Ayden, that you would be *my* Knight Commander, *my* second in command." Daemon stated slowly, evenly, making sure that Ayden caught the full implications of accepting this position. Ayden looked at Daemon and smiled, but for what other reason had Daemon groomed him for ten years before sending him to the Academy. Ayden was more than willing to play this role for Daemon.

      Daemon caught his look and smiled. Ayden returned the affectionate look with a pleased smile of his own. If ever there was a person Ayden would follow to the grave it would be this man. He held no delusions about Daemon being a fit mate or life partner for him. Ayden doubted either of them would survive such a relationship. Besides Daemon was like a brother to Ayden, a dear friend, nothing more than that.

"I take that as an acceptance of the position I am offering you." Ayden bowed his head and said.

"I would be honored Lord Daemon." Ayden pinned the medal to his sash and Daemon walked into the stables saying over his shoulder. "Come Knight Commander, if you are to go into battle you must have the equipment to see you through it." Ayden followed Daemon into the stable and to a stable block that held two magnificent war horses.

  Both of the magnificent beasts were black as melted pitch, but one was armored in barding decorated with wolves and the other in barding decorated with prowling panthers. Daemon bowed to the horses and moved to the one on his left, saying "This one is Nightshade, the other is Vitoria she will bear you to swift victory or die trying, and Vitoria is yours from this day forward." Ayden looked at the magnificent horse in the panther armor and approached gently. This horse was a Princely gift to be given. Daemon took him by the shoulder and turned him so that he was facing an armor stand with a set of heavy Knights armor upon it. It was similar to Daemons in the fact it was decorated. But it was decorated with panthers and vines, and the helm was that of a roaring panther, again the eye slits were the panthers open roaring mouth.

    Daemon helped Ayden into the heavy armor and Ayden grunted at the unfamiliar weight of it but he did not complain as he belted on his sword and tested out his mobility. The armor weighed far more than any mortal could bear, as it was thicker and made of sturdier steel to withstand the force of an Immortals blow. But his mobility was only slightly more restricted than it had been in the field armor that he had been wearing as a cadet. Daemon slipped his sash back over his head and checked him over carefully making sure everything was tightly fastened. He then mounted his horse Nightshade and motioned for Ayden to do the same. Ayden mounted Vitoria and held his helmet carefully in the crook on one arm as he steered the horse with the reins in his free hand and knees. As Daemon led the way back to the platoon he explained where they would be going and why. "...The Southern Border is under attack by the Southern Packs, their King, and your grandfather demands your fathers head and a sum of money he has fined us for 'harboring a criminal of his land'." Daemon said slowly Ayden frowned angrily, but continued to listen in silence. "When we failed to comply, they began attacking the south wall, the wall that separates our countries; my father has sent me to end the conflict by any means necessary." Ayden watched as Daemon's face spread into an eager grin tempting him to ask.

"And what are you going to do?" Daemon looked at Ayden and said very calmly and with a straight face.

"I am going to kill their King and take over the Southern Packs." Ayden did not doubt that Daemon would do all that he said and more.

Their conversation stopped abruptly when they reached the platoon. Daemon brought his horse about so that he was in front of the platoon, whom was now standing at attention and he spoke then his voice dead and cold.

"I will say this once and once only, I do not tolerate disobedience or mutiny in my soldiers." He growled at them leaning over the horn of his

saddle. "*Any* order I or Lord Ayden gives *will* be followed to the letter, there will not be exceptions, and death is the only recourse for disobedience." Daemon whirled his horse around and trotted back to Ayden and snapped.
"They have thirty minutes to be ready and formed up by the gate for our departure." Before he rode off again Ayden looked down at his horse's neck and smiled before barking at his platoon.
"Thirty minutes before departure, get your horses and get formed up by the gate!" With that his platoon was off running for the stables their heavy boots thudding against the cobblestones in a pleasant rhythm. Ayden rode off after Daemon and caught up with him by the gates where he was again talking to Commander Chase, this time with his helmet on. Ayden stopped a few yards away and blocked out the conversation. It was not any business of his what they were talking about.

    At the end of the thirty minutes Ayden's platoon was ready to depart, riding in ranks of five abreast and ten deep. Ayden inspected them before nodding to Daemon who was waiting to signal the guards at the top of the gates to open them. Daemon raised his arm and signaled to the guards at the top of the gate and the gates swung open with a protesting groan. Ayden signaled to his platoon as Daemon started the platoon out at a swift walk that developed gradually into a full-fledged gallop through the gates and out of the capital they thundered. They kept that pace throughout the day stopping only for brief rests and little bits of food, and carried a more moderate pace well into the night.

For four months they continued this, traveling by the swiftest roads towards the southern wall. Daemon and Ayden talked constantly, strategizing over maps and discussing battle plans well into the night when they made camp. Ayden was dead certain that he would follow Daemon no matter where the man led him. Be it into the very mouth of hell. He was sure that Daemon knew that as well, why else would he have spent so long grooming Ayden? When they came to the difficult pass that the mortals knew by the name of Dead Man's Pass, named so because no mortal had ever made it back through that pass alive. It took them three weeks to transverse this pass and come to the long valley that housed the wall. And looking down from on high Ayden was awed by the sight that was before him. The valley floor was covered in dark shapes moving about in block formations, and the mountains on either side had been carved into a magnificent city, Laochra Eíle, or better known as Warriors Rest.

    At the very mouth of the valley was the wall, which Ayden knew from his lessons at the Academy spanned the two hundred foot stretch between the mountains and rose three hundred feet into the air. At two hundred feet thick with only one entrance guarded by four gates that were only twenty feet tall and forty feet across. The gates themselves were formidable constructions. Built of three feet thick solid cured oak and plated by four inch thick steel plates and bared by solid beams of steel, operable only by a system of pulleys, cranks, and levers. But the wall was far from impenetrable; a determined army of Immortals could take the wall quite easily if they set their mind to it. There was a thundering boom that shook the valley and all activity on the field stopped. Daemon motioned for them to descend and began the descent into the valley.

Everywhere around them as they descended soldiers fell to their knees at the mere sight of Daemon shouting the traditional greeting to their Crown Prince and Regent. Ayden stayed close by Daemon's side as they rode through the soldiers Daemon came to a stop before a Knight dressed in the traditional Knight's armor bearing the traditional Knight Commander medal on his sash and spoke in a commanding voice.
"Knight Commander Roylce, report!" Daemon demanded of the startled Knight, who rose shakily to his feet and gave a hesitant report.
"...The Southern Packs men have broken through the first three gates, and they have attempted going over the wall but we have it thoroughly defended my Lord..." Daemon

nodded at the grim news and stood up in his stirrups looking around at the field of soldiers. "Roylce, gather your first officers and bring them here, Ayden arm the platoon with lances and set them a hundred yards from the gate then gather the rest of the troops." Daemon said calmly turning his horse about in a circle. Roylce growled and glared at Ayden and stepped forward spitting at the hooves of Ayden's horse. "I will not let this pup be in charge of any of the men stationed here, he has no authority over me or any of my men…" Daemon's response to Roylce's statement was immediate and violent cutting off any further words from the man. Ayden did not even have time to react as Daemon whipped his sword out of his sheath and speared Roylce through the heart with it. Piercing straight through the thick plates of Roylce's armor with a screech. As he gasped dying held up by Daemon as Daemon twisted the sword in his heart his face an expression of shock, Roylce tried to utter a protest but failed.

"I have no use for you then." Daemon snarled as the lights left Roylce's eyes. Roylce slid off the end of Daemon's sword as Daemon turned his attention to Ayden pointing to a decorated horn on Roylce's belt. "Grab that war horn off his belt and put it to good use I bet the soldiers are trained to respond to it, I will find the first officers and bring them out onto the field." Daemon said. Ayden nodded and slid out of the saddle of his horse to grab the horn and go through the Knight's belongings to see if there was anything else of use. Like a manual or something that would give him a clue on how many blasts on the horn and what notes he would have to do to summon the soldiers with any sense of urgency. He came across the Knights Compendium Immortalis and hurriedly flipped through it seeking the information that he was looking for. He found it near the back of the heavy tome, step by step instructions on how the soldiers were trained. Ayden read the several pages that this section took up and memorized them before taking the horn up. Climbing swiftly back into the saddle, Ayden nudged Vitoria into a quick trot. Before he began to sound the correct sequence of notes as he rode through the ranks of soldiers heading for the gates. His platoon followed after him in a thunderous gallop. The horn had a deep reverberating tone that carried through the valley and echoed across the city.

Within minutes of the first sounding of the horn, the first platoons of soldiers were formed a hundred yards away from the gates which shook every few seconds with a resounding boom. Ayden rode up and down the first line and inspected the soldiers shouting orders with all the authority that he could muster.
"PIKE'S UP FRONT! FORM UP! HORSES TO THE RIGHT FLANK! ARCHERS TO THE LEFT FLANK AND UP ON THE WALL!" Ayden commanded as he rode through the ranks. Immediately his platoon detached and rode to the right of the gates. Ayden rode to the back of the army. Once there he stopped in front of a Platoon Commander. "You! You and your men will bring lances to the mounted platoon on the right flank, and ensure that the arches on the left flank and wall have a steady supply of arrows!" Ayden ordered calmly, the platoon Commander

bowed his head and motioned to his platoon before saying.

"Yes Knight Commander." The platoon Commander and his platoon of sixty departed at a swift run to do what they had been commanded and Ayden returned to the front lines where Daemon was waiting.

He gave Daemon a report of where he had sent the men, just like they had planned. Daemon nodded and continued to brief the first officers on the battle plans he and Ayden had drawn up on the four month journey to this spot.

"...We will wait for the enemy to fill the field before us, which is when my Knight Commander will wind his horn and you two..."Daemon pointed to two of the first officers. "Will give the command for the archers to open fire and rain death from above and the left flank..." Daemon pointed to himself and continued to lay out the battle strategy. "On the second blast of the horn the platoon I rode in with and myself will charge down the valley wall from the right flank, at that time the archers on the left flank are to ascend the wall and prepare to defend it from any attack that might come from above." Daemon smiled wickedly and gestured to the rest of the first officers and Ayden. "...At the third sounding of the horn, my Knight Commander will lead the rest of the men into the main fray and we will drive the Southern Packmen back into their own lands before taking them from them." There was another earth shattering boom as the first officers rushed to take their positions.

  Ayden turned to his first officers and said very calmly speaking over the Guard of his helmet.
"The only way we succeed is if we keep our ranks tight, let your platoon Commanders know, I want minimal loss to our side, remember keep it tight and show no mercy for you will receive none." Ayden said before sending them off to their posts he took his place at the head of the army with his sword in his hand. They had arrived in the valley with the rising sun but now the sun was high and on the wane. The gates shuddered asunder the steel bar bent beyond repair falling to the ground with crash. With a

wild rush the Southern Packmen rushed through the gap in the heavy gates. Ayden watched them fill the field and raised the horn to his lips and let it sing a single deep clear ringing note as the mass of enemies charged at him and his force.

There was a second's pause before a cloud of black flew from above and the left raining upon the field in a thousand buzzing shafts of death. Momentarily halting the enemies' forward charge as the force was confused and suddenly very disorganized. Ayden blew the second note before the screams on the field could reach him and Daemon lead the platoon down the valley wall and crashed into the disorganized right flank of the invading army in an arrow head formation with devastating effect. Ayden sounded the horn for the final time before kicking Vitoria into a slow trot while the army marched behind, their voices singing in unison in the Immortal language, praising their Prince and singing of their coming victory. Quickening the pace Ayden raised his sword and joined in the song.

When Ayden's force actually met with the Southern Packs it was a slow but sure slaughter, not once did the northern army falter, their ranks remained tight, pushing the enemy before them back towards the gap in the gates. Ayden stayed a few yards ahead of the army cutting a bloody swath through the enemy lines straight to where Daemon was embroiled in battle, looking fearsome in his armor. Any wounded that Ayden and the front lines left behind were swiftly put out of their misery by the trailing troops of the army, the ones that had yet to have seen any real battle. As the sun was sinking in the west Ayden linked back up with Daemon and his platoon by the gate. Daemon dismounted and Ayden followed suit.

"Well met Lord Ayden!" Daemon said exuberantly, Ayden smiled in response to the normally stoic Daemon's excitement. "Nothing better than a good fight to keep you on your toes, is there?" Daemon's voice rolled with a thick accent that Ayden hadn't realized that he'd had. Ayden bowed his head.

"No Lord Daemon, there is nothing better than protecting your home." Ayden stated as Daemon clapped him on the shoulder and led him back to the fore of the lines where they began to lay waste to the enemy forces.

    Forcing them back into the tunnel and advancing with every step they took. Daemon and Ayden led the army through the tunnel driving the Southern Packmen before them. They worked excellently as a team, Ayden protecting Daemon and Daemon doing likewise for Ayden, simply out of respect for each other.

    It took them many hours to make their way to the end of the tunnel, leaving hundreds of bodies in their wake. But when Daemon and Ayden stood at the end of the tunnel at dusk, they saw a sea of men still before them. These men though were backing away from the blood soaked Northern Army and their two ferocious leaders. Until a deep voice commanded them to hold their ground. A man on a huge war horse came to the fore of the Southern Army and he roared a deep throbbing sound that echoed against their ears. Daemon stepped forward and roared back, his roar far more intimidating and menacing than the other man's. The man dismounted from his horse and drew his sword accepting Daemons challenge. Daemon snarled and charged forward discarding his sword.

Ayden stepped forward to retrieve it and watched as the scene unfolded. Daemon was literally coming out of his armor as he charged forward his form shifting and his armor falling off of him. He fought in his terrible beast form, which his opponent who was a Vampire from the smell of him was unable to do, putting his opponent at a terrible disadvantage. Daemon was far larger and far more vicious, rending his opponent's armor with only his claws and fangs. A feat that no normal Immortal should be able to accomplish, nevertheless Daemon was far from normal. Ayden winced as the man impaled Daemon through the chest but then chuckled as Daemon snapped the hilt off the blade and threw it at the Vampire with a mocking howl.

Unarmed and clearly outmatched the Vampire tried to flee into the ranks of the Southern Packmen, but Daemon bore him down in an ostentatious manner and ripped the life from him before roaring his victory at the remaining southern solders. With such a show of brutality, and over half their force dead the Southern Packmen quickly surrendered. Daemon stayed on his feet long enough to pull the blade from his chest and accept their surrender with a smirk before falling to his knees. Ayden rushed forward to catch him before his head hit the rocky ground. Looking Daemon over Ayden determined that the wounds that Daemon had sustained were not fatal, though still very serious. Ayden called for a stretcher and had Daemon borne away to a safer location while he sorted out the prisoners.

Volume One

Chapter Five

  Daemon was ready to ride the next day, his wound was not even close to healed. But he would not sit still. He wore his armor and stormed about the valley behind the wall preparing the troops for the coming invasion. Siege engines were disassembled and set upon wagons, the prisoners were loaded into carts, and the supply train was assembled. These were all pulled by teams of oxen. The force that Daemon was taking with him, a total of three of the four thousand men of the valley mounted their horses and prepared to set off. They were ready to ride out by midmorning the day after the battle for the wall had been won. Ayden rode with Daemon at the head of the army, bearing the Royal banner.

  They talked little as they day progressed, growing ever hotter and more humid the further south they went. The land they entered was unlike that of the north, it was for the most part a tangled forest save for the clay paved road that cut straight through it. It was the only paved road in the entire country, and it led directly to the capital city.

It took them a total of twenty three days to reach the capital city of the south, Urbem Leonum. It was a straight southern march from the wall, they encountered very few villagers along the way, and most encounters ended without too much trouble. In that time Ayden looked closely after Daemon, as he was the only one that Daemon allowed close enough to him to do so. As Daemon could not tend to his wound himself, Ayden did it for him, understanding the level of trust that was placed in him to do so. They had grown close in the four month ride to the wall, despite their differences in age. The battle of the wall had only strengthened their relationship. Ayden surveyed Urbem Leonum with an appraising look, most of the buildings were made of wood and clay, save for the palace, that was made of stone.

Daemon surveyed the land around the capital noting that it was teeming with soldiers. He sighed and motioned for Ayden to follow him.

"It is time to do something daring Lord Ayden, are you with me?" Daemon asked with a smirk, Ayden bowed his head with a small smile.

"I will follow you wherever you lead my Lord." Ayden stated calmly Daemon smiled and shook his head before saying lightly.

"Then come Lord Ayden, let us meet your grandfather and end this war." Daemon motioned for the army to stay still, only he and Ayden would move forward bearing a white banner.

  The southern pack soldiers parted way for them and allowed them access to Urbem Leonum. Under a white banner, they were not stopped even as they approached the palace. Once having reached the palace they were relieved of their weapons and escorted inside to see the King. Ayden memorized the route they took to the throne room, his head on a swivel and counting the amount of soldiers that prowled the halls of the palace. Once in the throne room he refused to even look at the man sitting on the throne until he had checked and memorized where each of the exits were located.

Just in case this turned into a shit show and they had to get out fast. The soldiers escorting them bowed to their King and departed. Ayden looked up at the man who sat high above them on a lofty dais upon a graven throne of black granite.

The King stared them down from his throne and beckoned Daemon forward, it was clear the gesture was meant for Daemon. As when the King looked at Ayden it was with a look of disgust. But Ayden did not leave Daemon's side and followed Daemon to the center of the room. He met the Kings hazel eyes and held them boldly, noting that this man looked very similar to Carmelito, only his features were somewhat harder. Like his personality was personified in his physical appearance. Ayden took a whiff of the man's scent and had to refrain from curling his lip in distaste, whereas Carmelito smelled of freshly turned earth, this man smelt of rotting fruit. This man also lacked the aura of softness that Carmelito had about him, this man was a hardened, heartless, killer.

"Lord Daemon you have a stray pup following at your heels, get rid of It." the King said softly his voice echoing through the room in a reverberating timbre.

Daemon cocked his head to the side and smiled he took off his helm and handed it to Ayden who tucked it under one arm.
"No King Aonghus I think Lord Ayden will stay with us, after all he has a vested interest in watching his grandfather fall." Daemon said calmly, Aonghus turned his attention to Ayden and looked him over.
"Show me then your form whelp of my son." Aonghus demanded Ayden snarled angrily and looked to Daemon. As far as Ayden was concerned the only person who could give him an order was Daemon. Daemon nodded his head to Ayden and took his helmet back. Ayden slowly removed his own head piece and allowed his form to shift into his half form and roared. His grandfather looked impressed for a split second before he waved his hand dismissively. "A panther, I could have made great use of you whelp I see my son chose to spare you for your

strength." Ayden shifted back and spun his helmet slowly in his hands.

"No, I do not think you could have grandfather, you see Carmelito did not spare me because of my strength, he spared me for one reason only." Ayden said slowly as he looked back up at Aonghus with a fierce glare. If there was anything in this world he hated then it would be people whom only looked at you on the surface. This fool had insulted Carmelito, and Carmelito was his family and Ayden was going to defend him. No matter what. "He spared me because he saw himself in me, he and I are more kin than you and he will ever be." Aonghus snarled and leaned forward in his throne looking ready to attack.

    Daemon held his hand up and brought Aonghus's attention back to him. He kept his tone light and mocking. Ayden knew what Daemon was doing. Trying to get the king all riled up, would make it easier to end this war. By a duel for the crown.

"I am sorry to interrupt this petty family quarrel but I am not here to settle this family squabble

Aonghus, I am here for your head and the crown that sits upon it." Daemon declared softly, Aonghus gave them a wicked smile and stood casting off his robes and revealing his body to be encased in heavy armor, far heavier than any normal Immortals armor. He tapped his crown and said.

"The only way you are getting this crown, boy, is if you pry it out of my cold dead hands." Aonghus stated with a cruel laugh then he tapped his breast plate and continued as he descended the dais steps. "I heard your half breed claws can rend Immortal steel, so I had this armor made especially for you, it is twice as thick as regular Immortal issue and made of a special alloy that allows it to remain light as a regular suit of armor but twice as strong." Ayden backed away from Daemon hearing his bones beginning to snap and break as the change came over him.

  Standing in his half form Daemon rolled his shoulders and cracked his knuckles as Aonghus drew his sword, it was a wicked looking blade, serrated from the cross piece to the tip which was broad and heavy, made for piercing armor. Ayden growled, ready to jump in and defend his prince and friend. But Daemon motioned for him to stay away, and much to Ayden's surprise spoke in the guttural language of the Immortals, his lupine snout made it difficult for him to speak, but manage it he did. Ayden grinned as Daemon spat a particular insult at Aonghus, but it was effective and brought the King roaring down the last steps at Daemon swinging his sword like a mad man.

  Daemon dodged the sword and laughed hurling insults at the heavily armored King all the while taking measured swipes at him leaving deep gouges in the thick metal. They traded glancing blows for many minutes before Daemon managed to rip Aonghus's breast plate away and lay the man open from shoulder to hip, blood splattered the ground and Daemon roared as Aonghus speared him with his blade, the sword sinking into his left shoulder with a screech and catching on his breast plate as Aonghus tried to withdraw, unable to do so he drove it through. Daemon howled in agony but pushed through the pain and brought his hands together on Aonghus's head. Unable to get proper purchase on the king's head, Daemon ripped the crown off throwing it to the side. As he dug his claws into the soft flesh of the Kings skull and began to squeeze.

    Ayden watched warily as Daemon's shoulders strained and the muscles in his arms, shoulders, and neck bunched and bulged with the effort. Aonghus growled through his teeth and tried to pry Daemon's hands away, but Daemon had a solid grip on him and snarling shook him off. With a wet snap the Kings jaw broke and his growling turned into low moans, seconds later there was a wet crack and like an over ripe melon Aonghus's head caved in coating Daemon's hands in gore. He roared his victory and stumbled backwards, Ayden went to him as Guards came pouring into the room, he scooped up the crown that was lying on the floor and placed it on Daemon's head. The guards stopped and approached warily. Ayden helped support Daemon and snarled in warning at the Guards.

"This was a fair challenge, kneel before the King." Ayden growled at them, hesitantly the guards got down on their knees and bowed. Daemon sagged against Ayden who half dragged, half carried Daemon up the dais steps to the throne. He snapped the hilt off the blade and pulled it the rest of the way through Daemon's shoulder causing Daemon to groan. Turning back to the guards he went down the dais until he was looming darkly over the kneeling men. He knew what Daemon would want him to do, secure the city.

That was what he had to do first, that was the main priority here, above all else even Daemon. "Raise the Northern Banner over the palace, Urbem Leonum has been taken in the name of the Emperor, send an emissary to the Northern Army to escort them into the city this war is over, and find me the best physician that Urbem Leonum has to offer." The men bowed their head with discontented looks but rushed off to follow his commands. Ayden returned to Daemon's side to find him slumped against the back of the throne unconscious but still breathing. Ayden reviewed his knowledge of medicine and found it irritably lacking, then he reviewed his knowledge of Daemon. Coming up with only one idea Ayden pulled off one of his bracers, Daemon needed mortal blood to sustain himself like a Vampire, though he was not one. What the blood of an Immortal would do for him, Ayden wondered as he bit into his wrist.

      Daemon was no longer just Ayden's idol, but his Commander, and infinitely more important than that, Ayden considered him a friend even if Daemon did not. Ayden brought his wrist up to Daemon's mouth, tilting his head back so he would not choke. For a few seconds there was no response, and then Daemon started to drink. The feeling was not painful, merely unpleasant as Ayden felt his strength being sapped away. The feeling of weakness brought Ayden to his knees as his vision flickered and went black. He could feel himself falling backwards down the dais steps and away from Daemon, but he never felt himself land.

Chapter Six

When Ayden woke he found himself lying at the bottom of the dais steps with Daemon standing over him looking at him with a fury that Ayden had never seen before. The look on Daemon's face chilled Ayden to his core. It took Daemon a long time to form a coherent sentence he was that furious with Ayden.
"Do you have any idea what you have done? Any idea just how close to death you just came? Never do that again!" Daemon growled angrily at him, Ayden tried to sit up but failed as his arms had not the strength to support him. Daemon met his eyes and very coldly said. "I do not want the blood of another friend on my hands whether they be willing or not." It was at that moment that a portly little man, by the smell of him a vampire, however under that was an underlying lingering musk scent, like willows in the fall.

He came into the room escorted by a couple of guards. He immediately rushed to Ayden's side seeing as how Ayden was the one lying on the floor. Daemon stepped away and let him work.

"You are a Lycanthrope, yes? What breed?" the little man asked Ayden as he pulled various instruments out of a heavy wooden case that the Guards had carried in and set down next to him, he put his fingers to Ayden's throat to feel for his heartbeat and counted the beats as Ayden responded.

"Were-panther, black, and turned by Lord Carmelito if you need specifics." The physician worked Ayden over and stopped at his wrist.

"Were you willing when you gave up your blood or was it forcefully taken?" he asked after a length, Ayden sighed and looked at Daemon, noting how easily Daemon was moving now. He had made the right choice and he would happily do it again.

"I was willing and it was more than worth it." Ayden said with a chuckle making Daemon growl in frustration. The physician sighed and pulled a large jar of dried herbs from his case and handed it to Ayden saying.

"Take a pinch of this every couple of hours, and your strength should return within a few days you should also stay at rest during this time." The physician turned to Daemon and spied the gash in his armor. "Remove your breast plate your majesty, or I should say Prince Vladimir the second." Daemon stopped unbuckling his breast plate and looked up with a deathly glare.
"How do you know that name? Who are you?" Daemon growled at the physician.

Who held his hands up in a gesture of surrender before giving Daemon a bemused smile and explaining himself.
"I never forget a scent and I brought yours into this world, I am the former Royal physician of the Northern Empire Albert Von Sewdan." The little man said. Daemon frowned thoughtfully and finished taking off his breast plate. He barred his chest, revealing the now almost fully healed wound in the center of his right pectoral muscle, and the fresh and fast healing wound just below his left collar bone. Albert shook his head and motioned for Daemon to sit as he went back to his chest and brought forth a bottle of

amber liquid saying. "Hold still, I am going to disinfect the wound while I still can, this is Wolfs Brew, I am sure you are familiar with the drink yes?" Daemon nodded and Albert uncorked the bottle and poured the liquid over Daemon's shoulder making him hiss and snarl. When Albert was done he handed Daemon the bottle and let him take a gulp. Ayden knew that the potent drink was made from aconite or wolfs bane which could also be a poison if brewed correctly.

He personally had never had the drink before, but knew it was brewed by Immortals for Immortals and knew it to be potent enough to kill most mortals that drank it by mistake. When Albert was done with Daemon he returned to Ayden who was struggling to pop the cork out of the jar that held his herbs. Albert popped the cork and took out a large pinch of the herbs and stuck it between Ayden's lips and teeth instructing him to chew but not swallow any of the herbs. The herbs were foul tasting but Ayden chewed them slowly and deliberately anyways. Albert packed up his chest and sat upon it.

He crossed his left ankle over his right knee and looked from Ayden to Daemon who was putting on his tunic and breast plate again. Daemon sent the guards scurrying from him with a few orders. Four came and picked Ayden up from where he was laying and bore him off to another part of the palace. Ayden did not have the presence of mind to memorize the route back to the throne room, his head was still groggy. Thanks to the herbs Ayden was gaining a little strength back though.

By the next morning Ayden could walk about on his own, though not for very far. Daemon kept Ayden close by his side as the days passed, Ayden understood why. Now that Daemon had control of the Southern Packs, he would have to subjugate them to his father's rule, and that would cause a lot of ire amongst the people. The first thing that Daemon did as King was send decrees of the new laws out to all the provinces of the southern Kingdom. Ayden helped Daemon by organizing the patrols of Urbem Leonum and helping maintain the Emperors laws within the city. Even though he was still weak, Ayden proved he had strength enough for this. The days passed into weeks, and weeks passed into months. It was a hard struggle a daily fight with the people that often ended in bloody riots in the streets.

Ayden was hard pressed to find a way to keep the peace. He tried everything in his power to keep it. But it was to no avail, blood was spilt nearly every day over the most pointless of things. As if thing's were not bad enough, Ayden had to foil several attempts on Daemon's life, and his own besides and Ayden was less than merciful with them. Any threat on Daemon's life was a threat upon Ayden himself. Since Ayden viewed Daemon as his alpha and close friend, his brother of battle and blood.

Within a year, Daemon had most of the outlying regions under control, though the capital was still in open revolt. Ayden increased the amount of patrols in the city, and he himself participated in the patrols. Daemon was determined they would have the Southern Packs completely under the northern Empire's rule before the next year was out. No matter the cost, even if that included taking the children of the Southern Packs Nobles to be raised in the houses of the north. Ayden knew that Daemon was almost to that point, as much as he hated the idea of separating families. Daemon might be a cold man but he was a man with unbending morals, and family was something of overbearing importance to him.

Ayden knew this; he had seen Daemon when Daemon was reading his father's letters. Sitting hunched on his throne rereading the same parchment scroll over and over by candle light. As little as Daemon saw his father he still cared deeply for the man though he would not show it in the slightest. They were in the middle of one such conversation when a messenger arrived from Daemon's father. It was a decree for Daemon to begin sending the young Nobles of the Southern Courts to the north to be thoroughly educated in the ways of the Empire without interference of the children's parents. The decree had Daemon snarling in anger, and Ayden agreed.

"...This will cause a lot of ire with the southern Nobles, and animosity will spring from the children when they are taken from them." Ayden stated slowly as Daemon leaned on the table looking over the decree again.

"Aye, this will be difficult, how to separate the children from the parents without causing animosity or grief? The parents will be easy to deal with, but the children not so, they will feel singled out since it's just noble children being sent off..." Daemon said with a growl. Daemon ran his hands through his hair and sighed. "I have a plan Ayden to nip the panic in the bud we will relocate all the children equally, common and noble alike. To the academy not to any noble families." Ayden cocked his head to the side and pondered it for a bit, he eventually came to the same conclusion as Daemon had. He thought about it some more, wondering where the parents would fit in.

"What about the parents sire? How do we get them to give up the children willingly?" Ayden asked after a long moment of silence. Daemon looked at him with a wicked grin.

"Oh I have my ways, they will be reluctant, but they will give up their children." Daemon said lightly. He spoke no more of his plans and Ayden would not ask anything else of him. He did not want to know what little scheme was going on in Daemon's mind at that moment. After all he knew that he would without a doubt be involved in it sooner rather than later.

The situation with the children was solved in a rather simple manner, the children were gathered up and sent to the academy, and their parents were given the option of seeing their children again in a few years or never again as they would be stripped of land and title and regulated to the ranks of a common soldier and sent off to battle and when they returned to it would be to only to glimpse their child in all their glory as a noble of the Empire.

It was a miracle how readily most of the nobles agreed after that. The children though proved a bit harder to break into the way of the Northern rule, at least the older ones were. Daemon had to constantly read letters of complaint from the Northern Nobles about two trouble makers. Eoan and Aeon, a set of twin were-ravens, though no one actually knew if they were siblings or not. Their father had died in the battle for the wall, and their mother had died of grief shortly after she had learned of her mate's death. Those two trouble makers Daemon had them sent back to him personally and took them under his own wing for a few years before sending them off to the Academy. With the two ring leaders of the children's rebellion now reformed. Things were progressing much smoother for them.

Volume One

Chapter Seven

It took a total of six years for Daemon to conquer the Southern Packs. To convert them to the rule of his father and with pride he handed his crown to his father on bended knee. Ayden watched him with admiration and was awarded his just dues for his participation in the takeover of the Southern Kingdom. He was awarded the position of Daemon's First Knight, but it was not without sacrifice. His father Carmelito was opposed to the appointment, and they fought bitterly over it.

"You have no idea what kind of man Lord Daemon truly is!" Carmelito roared at his son having arrived a few days after Ayden's appointment as First Knight, Ayden shrugged him off and replied softly.

"Trust me father I know exactly who I am dealing with." His father stormed away from him for a second before coming back at him with double fury.

"That proves exactly how much you do not know the man you are serving!" Carmelito snarled angrily. Ayden snarled in return and pushed back with his words.

"Father please! Daemon is my friend, my ally, I trust him despite what he may have done in the past." Ayden pleaded, his father ran a hand over his face and shook his head.

"You can't do this, you are far more merciful than Lord Daemon, far kinder, and you know this even if you have buried it within yourself!" Carmelito growled at him poking his finger at Ayden. "Where is the man who cried at the sight of the falling moon as he lay dying?" Ayden locked his father in a deadly glare and snarled. "That man has had to put his personal feelings aside in order to survive father and became the man you see before you now." Ayden pushed his father aside and stormed away, feeling furious with himself.

But refusing to look back at his father's hurt expression. His father called after him. "There will come a day Ayden when you will regret following after him!" Ayden paused mid-step as he heard his father whisper. "And when that day comes I will be there waiting for you to return home." But he forced himself to continue walking away from his father; he was Daemon's First Knight, an enforcer of the Emperor's laws. That was the path that he had chosen for himself, if his father could not accept that then so be it. It was painful to fight with his father over this, but Ayden would not change his mind.

    He returned to Daemon's side, proud of what he had accomplished, but saddened by the fact he had disappointed his father. Daemon did not give him any rest he just put him to work preparing for their departure from the southern lands. There was much to do, and now that he was First Knight he had much to learn, first of all about being a Royal Knight, and then about Daemon's work as Regent and what that entailed for him

    Leaving the southern lands, Ayden rode beside Daemon, his new armor weighing heavily on him, only because he was unaccustomed to it. Daemon too wore new armor, similar in make to his previous armor but made of a lighter, stronger alloy. Ayden knew that Daemon had made both sets of armor, perfecting the alloy mixture to make a light yet suitably stronger metal for his and Ayden's armor. Even Daemon's claws could not pierce this metal, and his claws could pierce most things including average Immortal steel. Daemon had learned the formula from Aonghus's Royal smiths and had perfected it in the time that he had spent in Urbem Leonum.

    They talked animatedly, Daemon beginning the many lessons that Ayden would have to learn to take his proper place as First Knight. Ayden absorbed the lessons eagerly; they could only do so much on the road though and Ayden was eager to begin the lessons he could not learn while on the road. At night they sparred furiously, keeping in top form and health.

    Six months of travel by the broad roads brought them back to Daemon's estate where Ayden's lessons began in earnest. Daemon let more of himself go with Ayden allowing Ayden to get closer to him than anyone else had in many years. Not since Aodhan's death had he allowed anyone this close. He even allowed Ayden to read his Compendium in length, explaining things to Ayden in detail that Ayden did not understand. Such as the trial of the shamed, and what it meant to have undergone it.

"For those of us that are a rarity amongst our peers Ayden it is difficult to rise to their expectations or even above." Daemon said on night over a glass of Wolfs Brew. Ayden was surprised by the fact that he liked the bitter drink. More surprised was he to learn that Daemon drank it regularly. "To even survive is a challenge because we are either so frowned upon or have so many expectations piled upon us that we are forced to either succeed or die." Ayden nodded in agreement, it had been that way at the Academy when the instructors had realized that he was a were-panther.

   Their expectations of him had been so high that the pressure had been almost unbearable, he had not lived up to the high expectations nor had he even exceeded them thanks to his abrasive personality. Though he had excelled at the Academy in ways that the other cadets did not he failed to rise to the specific expectations of Commander Chase, though he rose to meet and exceed Daemon's apparently. Commander Chase wanted a soldier that would be loyal to the Emperor and to the Emperor only. Ayden had made it very clear from the very beginning whom his allegiance was to, and to whom it would always be. As far as Ayden was concerned Daemon was his Alpha, therefore he was his Lord and master and the only one he needed to obey. Though the reality of it was by serving Daemon he was serving the Emperor.

    Ayden learned quickly under Daemon's strict tutelage taking less than three years to master all that was required of him. He learned the ins and outs of the Courts and fine-tuned his political game. Daemon put Ayden in charge of the Knights of the Royal Guard and his surveillance agents. Ayden was nothing less than thorough with his duties with the Knights and agents. As such he was amassing quite the sinister reputation, one that mirrored Daemon's own reputation. It seemed that Ayden's reputation would grow boundlessly and far exceed Daemon's except for the fact that Daemon's own dark reputation was continuously growing.

    Whenever either Ayden or Daemon's names were mentioned, in passing or in official matters people cringed and looked over their shoulders. It was this fear of him that Daemon encouraged as he dealt with the criminals of the Immortal world in such a manner as to inspire such terror that the laws would not be broken again for a long period of time. Ayden aimed to achieve such a reaction in his every day dealings with the Nobles of the court, and with the Knights under his command. He inspired fear and respect wherever he went, nearly in the same respect as Daemon did. Often when the pair was together, their presence was so commanding and intimidating that no others dared to even speak to them, save for a select few.

    Those few were Daemon's father, Daemon's mother, whom Ayden recognized as the Alpha from the Trial of the Cubs, and the last person whom dared to speak openly in the commanding presence of both Ayden and Daemon was Commander Chase. Kain, held no qualms about talking openly in front of any one, so the withered little vampire assassin did not impress Ayden all that much. Though Ayden did respect the man a great deal, Kain could kill him a thousand different ways and never get caught.

    On one such occasion was a Royal banquet held in honor of Daemon's two hundred and seventeenth year of life. Daemon insisted that Ayden sit on his right hand side at the banquet table, a position of the highest honor among the court Nobles. It was the position taken by the Beta of the pack, or the steward of a coven. A seat that any respecting noble of the Courts would have killed to have, but Daemon gave it to Ayden who took the seat and boldly engaged in conversation with Daemon's parents no other noble dared enter into the conversation. Ayden ate and drank alongside Daemon, though the night rapidly digressed into talk about their duties as Regent and First Knight it was only then that the other Nobles joined into the conversation. When the night came to an end

Ayden left the banquet with a lovely Lady on his arm a conversation partner nothing else, the same as Daemon had a few hours before.

Ayden smiled to himself as he thought of the next day's work, he enjoyed his work with Daemon. Though he did not necessarily enjoy all the aspects of his work as Daemon's First Knight, but it was a duty that he would not deviate from. This was a path he had chosen for himself because this is what he felt was right.

Volume One

Chapter Eight

It was rare to see Daemon without Ayden at his side, though the pair could work independently of each other and did so often. As the Commander of the Royal Guard Ayden was flawless, executing his duties perfectly. Just as Daemon had trained and groomed him to. Ayden was a smart and resourceful man, handling the intelligence agents that Daemon put under his command was a challenge though not impossible. As the time passed Daemon added more responsibility to Ayden's plate. Giving him various businesses to manage and build while also completing his tasks as First Knight to Daemon, the world was changing around them, spears and swords were becoming obsolete replaced by pistols, muskets, and cannons.

All these things were mortal creations spurred on by a new blossoming era of innovativeness and industry. The Immortal world had as of yet to employ these weapons but it was only a matter of time. Ayden worked himself ragged day in and day out without complaint trying to prove himself capable in Daemon's eyes. He pushed himself to the utmost limit of his endurance in the pursuit of his duties to Daemon. Pacing around his office Ayden looked at the parchment before him. On it was a list of names, and with it came a dozen or so detailed sketches. These were the individuals Ayden was tasked with finding and carrying out Immortal justice upon. All of them had broken Immortal law in some manner, and their sentences were ready to be carried out. Ayden just had to find them first. It was while Ayden was pacing in his office that a young Knight entered and bowed to him.

"Lord Ayden, you have been called to the feeding hall Lord Hareth has challenged you." The Knight stated slowly. Ayden snarled in anger hand going instantly to his sword.

"On what grounds?" He demanded, the Knight backed away and bowed again, fearing that Ayden would slay him in his enraged state.

"The Lord Hareth says you cannot take proper form, and thus are unfit to lead the Knights, unfit to hold the title of First Knight to the

Regent." The Knight stated keeping his head low, he hesitantly added as he reached for the door. "He says you are a disgrace to the Lycanthrope race boasting of how you are a mighty panther when you can't even take on a proper form." Ayden snarled and moved out from behind his desk.

"And do you believe him?" Ayden asked his voice dangerously low, the Knight gulped and shook his head.

"No my Lord, but a great many of the Knights do as none of them have ever seen your form." The Knight said quickly. Ayden pushed past the Knight and stormed through the halls of the Knights headquarters.

He quickly came to the feeding hall and pushed through the great oaken doors and into the room. The doors slammed into the walls on either side of him and brought all attention on him and silence to the boisterous hall. Ayden looked around the room and let the distaste show on his face as he surveyed the Knights around him. Deadly calm Ayden spoke to the room.

"Lord Hareth, I hear you have come to question my right to lead these men not based on my ability to lead them but because you are under the impression that I lack a form." Ayden cocked his head to the side flexing his hands by his sides as he surveyed the room. "You called me out to challenge me Lord Hareth so show yourself, you say I am unfit show me that you are better!" He roared into the silence of the room. Slowly a man at the end of the room rose to stand; his armor was of fine make, as was his sword. But they were nothing compared to the armor that Ayden wore, or the sword that Ayden bore.

    The man stood cockily one hand on his sword, the other gesturing in the air as he talked. His speech was slurred and his face was slightly flushed, like he'd imbibed far too much. But Ayden was not going to let this pass as some drunken fools ramblings. No this was obviously a long time in the making.

"Aye I challenge ye Ayden the formless, and I'll be the one taking yer title and lands." The man said with a chuckle. Ayden gave a grim smile and drew his sword and pointed it at Lord Hareth.

"You want to see my form, then I will show it to you, but it will be the last thing you ever see." Ayden snarled as he dropped his sword, his armor fell off him as his form contorted and shifted into his full panther shape. With a roar Ayden stood before all the men in the feeding hall in all his glory. He flexed his powerful muscles as he looked up at Lord Hareth's shocked face and tamped down his back legs preparing to spring. Lord Hareth got maybe three feet before Ayden brought him down in a single bound.

Ayden hooked his claws under the lip of Hareth's breast plate and ripped the overly decorated piece from him. Leaving his chest and stomach fully exposed to Ayden's cruel claws and fangs. Ayden set one paw on the man's chest and dug his claws in with a growl as he locked eyes with Lord Hareth. Who knew that he was going to die a very slow very painful death Ayden could see it in the frightened look in Hareth's eyes.

Rising from his kill Ayden padded away from the gory mess and back to his armor and sword. There was a soft chuckle and Ayden's head snapped up and he saw Daemon's figure in the doorway of the feeding hall. Ayden immediately bowed his great head and growled in welcome. A response that was reciprocated as Daemon dipped his head to Ayden in return. Daemons action gave a clear show of the trust and friendship he held with Ayden. A bond of mutual respect and loyalty between them both. Daemon beckoned to Ayden and left, Ayden shifted and gathered his belongings before following not liking the grim look that had been on Daemon's face. He followed Daemon to his office. Daemon took a seat by Ayden's grand desk and waited for Ayden to sit down before he began to speak.

"I have received word of an immortal rampaging through human villages at random, killing as he pleases." Daemon said slowly, his eyes never left Ayden and Ayden could feel his heart sink as he figured where exactly this was going. "None so far have lived long enough to give us enough information to find and capture the Immortal." Ayden shook his head in disgust but listened impatiently for the rest of Daemon's news.

He knew there was a reason that Daemon was telling him this personally instead of in a missive or letter.

"I am sorry to be the bearer of bad news Ayden but your mortal family has been slain..." Daemon's sentence was cut off by Ayden slamming his fist into the nearest wall, his skin split over his knuckles and blood welled up from the wounds. Fury was his first response, to build a wall of anger and deny everything. It only lasted for a few seconds though before reason began to break it down. He should have been prepared for his family to die. He was Immortal they were not. They would have died regardless, it was their fate and his love and pride prevented him from putting them through the same torment he'd undergone to become what he had. But this was different, his mortal family hadn't died naturally as they should have, they had been murdered, murdered by another Immortal. He turned to Daemon and growled.

"What would you have me do my Lord?" Daemon cocked his head to the side and smiled wickedly baring his long fangs in the light.

"Everything in your power to find this Immortal that so brashly broke my father's laws." Daemon stated calmly. Ayden bowed his head to Daemon and licked at his wounded hand before saying.

"It will be my pleasure Lord Daemon to do this for you." Daemon bowed his head to Ayden and stood, he clapped Ayden on the shoulder and his expression softened for a moment.

"There is nothing more important than family in this world, I will make sure that your family is avenged." Daemon stated before walking out of Ayden's office.

Ayden watched him go before growling angrily. He followed after and found five young Knights and sent them to mobilize the others. He was going to find this Immortal that was rampaging through the human villages and he was going to bring him before Daemon dead or alive.

Volume One

Chapter Nine

Ayden rode through every ruined village that had been hit by the marauding Immortal. He took in every sight and smell that wafted too him from the carnage strewn village. Ayden collected all the evidence he could, and had his men bury the dead. Everywhere about these villages hung the smell of fetid meat and it was not the foul smell of rotting corpses. But a thick and heavy scent like the Immortal had marked his territory before leaving the place. Ayden memorized the scent so that he would never forget it. He let the images of the slain villagers be burned into his mind to remind him of what he was hunting. This monster, the man that had done this had no remorse for what he had done.

It took Ayden ten years of following the villain's path of slaughter to grow sick of the sights that he was seeing and return to his home at the Knight's headquarters in Coelum. Daemon was there for him through it all, a silent support that Ayden could lean on for strength and look to for direction. As Ayden had made him his Alpha, Daemon saw it as his duty to look after Ayden. To support him no matter the cost.

At night when Ayden slept the faces of the victims that had been slain haunted him. Begging Ayden for justice for relief and peace from their suffering. This forced Ayden to hunt harder and longer for the nameless Immortal that was causing so much chaos throughout the land. Ayden sent his men scouring the cities and towns for miles around for the next five years and there was not a single peep from the rampaging Immortal. Ayden increased the guard and Knights presences in the cities and towns across the land and for the next two decades there was peace. Ayden thought that the mindless massacres had ended for good.

At the end of those twenty years there was an uprising in the capital that forced Ayden to recall his forces to defend Coelum and send forces to quell the following rebellions in the south. Within three years, reports of whole village massacres came flooding back onto

Ayden and Daemon's desks. And they both were at a loss as what to do about it.

With the restarting of the murderous rampaging through the country side Ayden longed to send his men out to patrol the towns and cities in a show of force. But he could not in case there was a reoccurrence of rebellions that brought danger to the capital city. Ayden could often be found pacing in his office of the Knight's headquarters, or at Daemon's estate strategizing. For nearly five decades Ayden chased down every lead he could on the elusive Immortal that was rampaging through the countryside of the Empire. But the man as they had determined the Immortal to be was a ghost. There were only whispers of him in the wind and nothing more.

In this time Ayden grew more aggressive and violent, it was like the last of his humanity had been stripped away. Carmelito tried on several occasions to try and reconcile with Ayden. But Ayden would have none of it. He would neither listen nor care for what his father said to him, he was cold to the world. In matters of work and duty he was nothing less than efficient, flawless some would say. Ayden was given various other assignments other than the Immortal that he was chasing with such fervor and he hunted his targets down mercilessly. Though Ayden never got any closer to his true mark he did make great progress on his other marks, bringing them one by one before Daemon.

    It was during one night while Daemon and Ayden were discussing strategy and drinking at Daemon's estate that they received a rather unexpected visitor late in the night. They were hunched over Daemon's desk surveying maps of the Empire and discussing in low tones their next course of action when there was a soft knocking upon the study door. A thin man, whom Ayden had only seen a few times before and took to be Daemon's man servant entered, the ever cunning Kain.
"My Lord there is a young Lady here who wishes to speak with you." The man stated with a bow of his head. Daemon glanced up at the man and asked softly.

"Is it something important Kain? Or can it wait until a little later?" the man, Kain shook his head and said with another bow.
"No my Lord, I am afraid this is terribly urgent." Ayden backed away from the desk warily, wondering what Daemon was going to do, he hated to be interrupted.

    Daemon sighed and waved his hand dismissively. Hopefully this young lady had something worth troubling Daemon about. Ayden himself was irritated but it was nothing compared to how irritated Daemon could be if his focus was hampered by this interruption. "Send the lass in and we will see if what she says is indeed worth anything." He said to Kain who bowed and left quickly. They did not have to wait long before he was leading a short young Lady into the study.

    The young woman had long pale blond hair and grey blue eyes; every inch of her exposed skin was covered in tattoo's save for her face and hands, she was dressed in a sleeveless linen tunic and leather breeches, her feet were bare. She was beautiful in her own right, Ayden could give her that much. But there was something distinctly wild and fierce about her that made Ayden considerably wary of her. She was like a gust of wind, which could not be caught. That was Ayden's first impression of the young lady whom approached them so casually. As if she had not a single thing to fear from them.

  The girl bowed, not the traditional curtsy of the noble ladies of the Courts. Her movements were fluid like a dancers would be. Her voice was soft and melodic, with a rough timber undertone that made her voice pleasant to hear as she spoke.

"Forgive my sudden intrusion Crown Prince Daemon, Lord Ayden, but I believe that I have information that you seek." She said as she rose from her bow. Daemon nodded his head to her with an appraising look. He came out from behind the desk and stood before her. Towering over her as he was twice her height for the most part, he folded his arms across his chest and said with a slow growl.

"Tis forgiven for the moment, but it seems that you know more of me and mine than I know of you." The girl bowed her head and met Daemon's eyes challengingly before saying in a clear voice.

"I am Frostlilly De Lune, the youngest daughter of Commander Chase De Lune, and the twin sister of the man that you are pursuing so relentlessly." Ayden growled angrily, and Daemon stood up straighter his eyes lighting up in interest.

"What do you mean by that?" Daemon asked slowly. Frost bowed her head before she raised her chin proudly baring her throat to Daemon as she looked Daemon dead in the eye as she said.

"Exactly as I said, I am the sister of the man you are pursuing." Daemon waved his hand in a dismissing manner and said.

"I pursue any number of men and women on any given day." Frost smiled and withdrew a tattered tunic from her belt pouch, it was stained with blood. The blood of mortals, Ayden could still find the distinctive scent of fetid meat on the tunic, despite how it was cloaked by Frost's fresh scent.

This tunic obviously belonged to the man that had been rampaging through the countryside Ayden could not mistake that stench, not for the life of him, not anywhere. Fetid and foul, it was the stench of murder. She tossed it to Daemon and crossed her arms over her chest in a defensive manner.
"This is my evidence that my brother is your man, the Lycanthrope that has been killing at random." Frost said coolly. Daemon sniffed the tunic and nodded, he let it drop to the desk and his voice rumbled forth like thunder.
"This alone is not enough to prove that he was the one that murdered all those people merely that he was there." Daemon stated Ayden knew that Daemon was fishing for more information, something solid he could nail Frost's brother with. Also her, if she turned out to be implicit with the killings.

Frost nodded her head and gave a small sad smile like she knew exactly what he was doing. After all who was going to believe her on a tunic scrap and her words alone, it was now her word over her brothers, unless she could provide further proof of her brothers wrong doings.

"If only that were true, if you go to our family villa and search it you will find in my brothers room a Compendium Immortalis." Frost said hesitantly. "He took it from his very first kill and has been using since to record his deeds." Daemon cocked his head to the side at the new revelation and motioned for Frost to continue and with a weary smile she did.

"...The book will be hidden in a drawer beside his bed, and you will find him at our home in the city." Frostlilly continued to explain how she'd come about this information. It was not easy for her to reveal to them that she'd had no idea of her brothers hunting activities until quite recently. However the second she was sure, she had come to them to report it. Ayden could spot no lie in her eyes. Nor did she seem afraid of them. Only the stupid and the innocent walked willingly into the lion's den without fear.

Daemon looked over to Ayden and nodded. Ayden bowed his head understanding what he was to do. Touching Frost's shoulder he said.

"Take me there and show me." Ayden said softly. Frost nodded and followed him out the door, just as they were leaving Daemon asked.

"Your brother, what is his name?" Frost looked over her shoulder and said softly.

"Callain, my brother's name is Callain." Her tone was sad, but determined.

It was a long and silent ride to the Immortal capital city, Coelum. When they reached the sprawling metropolis Frost took the lead as Ayden summoned his Knights to him. They reached the mansion that Frost called home; a guard looked through the gate and hurried to open the gates for them crying.

"Lady Frost! Where have you been and why are you accompanied by the Lord Ayden and his Knights?" Frost looked at the man and dismounted. Ayden followed suit as Frost went to the guard and ordered him to find her father, Ayden waited in the court yard for Commander Chase to appear. The tiny man had retired from the Academy just after Ayden had graduated. Commander Chase came storming out of the villa and straight to Ayden who was waiting for him with his orders in hand. The orders were official, written and sealed with Daemon's seals of office. When the Commander held his hand out for the orders Ayden handed them over without even a hesitation.

When Commander Chase read the orders his face paled and his pale blue grey eyes grew hard.
"You want to search my home? On what grounds?" He demanded, Frost came forward and put a hand on her father's arm and muttered something under her breath to him. Commander Chase glared down at her and snarled. "Get inside we will discuss this matter in detail later." Ayden watched her go, to Frost's credit she walked away with her head held high. Cocking his head to the side Ayden turned his attention back to Commander Chase who was watching his daughter go with a tired look on his face. He held his hand out for his orders and motioned to his Knights.

"Commander Chase, I am truly sorry to invade the privacy of your pack and family, but it must be done." Ayden stated as he set his Knights into motion, he himself was going to search Callain's quarters, "If you could show me where your son Callain resides in this magnificent villa, I would greatly appreciate it." Commander Chase blanched but nodded and beckoned for Ayden to follow him before leading the way inside.

Frost was waiting just inside the door and she bowed her head to her father, before moving just ahead of them and leading the way further into the villa. Frost came to a standstill by an elaborately carved door that was bound with wrought iron. She bowed to both Ayden and her father as Ayden opened the door and entered the room. Inside the room was immaculate; Ayden had only seen one other room like it, Daemon's study. Ayden did a quick overview of the room before beginning his true search where Frost had told him to begin. Commander Chase stood at the entrance way with his arms folded over his chest and a tight frown on his face. Ayden ripped through the drawers by Callain's neatly made bed, tossing the contents about the room and inspecting the drawers and their respective cubbies thoroughly.

It took him several hours of minute inspection but he eventually found where Callain had built a compartment into the bottom of one of the drawers. After a few minutes of finagling Ayden popped the compartment open and found within as Frost had promised a worn and bloodstained Compendium Immortalis. Ayden opened the book up and flipped through it to where the handwriting transitioned from a straight and informal handwriting, to smooth and very formal script. Quickly Ayden read through it and his face grew hard as he read. He walked over to Commander Chase and thrust the book at him and growled.

"Did you know about your son's hunting activities?" Commander Chase read through a few paragraphs and tossed the book on the ground in disgust.

"I did not." He said raising his chin defiantly. There was a commotion in the hall as a tall well-built blonde young man who smelled strongly of fetid meat came across Frost, Ayden retrieved the book from the floor and headed for the door with every intention of arresting the young man who Frost identified as Callain as she called out to him to stop.

"...Wait Callain...Stop...Wait!" She cried, there was a sudden snarling sound and the smell of blood as Frost cried out and fell into the room holding her face. The youth stepped into the room with bloodied claws. Commander Chase stepped towards his son as Ayden drew his sword.

Callain licked at the blood off his clawed hand and smiled at Ayden wickedly.

"So you finally found me? No thanks to her no doubt, she always had an eye on me." Callain said pointing at his sister. He leaned over her picking her up by the throat and growled. "One of these day's dear sister, I am going to come back and I am going to kill you for what you have done." Ayden started forward swinging his sword, only to have it blocked by Commander Chase. Ayden growled at him as he saw Callain slip away back into the hall.

"What are you doing? Your letting him get away!" Commander Chase growled back softly.

"He is my son; I cannot stand by and let you kill him!" Ayden pushed the man away and sheathed his sword; he went after Callain only to find a trail of dead bodies left in the youths wake Knights and household servants alike.

Snarling furiously he returned to Callain's room and bent over Frost looking her over, she had three vertical gashes running down the right side of her face. They were ragged and bleed profusely. Ayden feared that Frost's right eye would be closed forever, as her eyelid was nearly shredded, to her credit she neither cried out or whined as he inspected her. He turned to Commander Chase and growled.

"Get me some linen or something so that I can stop this bleeding." Commander Chase stiffened and stalked away.

"For the sake of my pack I cannot have her here; they will kill her for betraying her brother." Commander Chase said coldly. "You can do whatever you want with her, from this moment forward she is exiled from my pack." Ayden looked up at him in shock; the Commander had just disowned his daughter because she had obeyed the law? In what right world did that make sense? Ayden helped Frost to her feet where she bowed to her father and walked out of the room with a straight back, not once did she falter or stumble. Ayden followed after her glaring at Commander Chase the entire time.

Helping Frost onto her horse Ayden looked up at her and bowed. He felt an overwhelming respect for this woman.
"To do what you have done took a great deal of courage Lady Frost. I would be honored to call you a comrade if you ever have the desire to join another pack." Ayden stated boldly, Frost gave him a small smile and turned her horse about.
"I would be honored to call you my brother Lord Ayden, but that is up to your Alpha isn't it?" Frost asked, Ayden climbed into his saddle and turned his horse about.
"Then let us go ask him." Ayden stated as he started forward leading Frost out into the city.

Volume One

Book Three

Family Bonds

Volume One

Prelude

Frost looked at her scarred visage in the small hand mirror she kept beside the bed. The vivid purple scars reminding her of the day she had been exiled by her father for betraying her brother three decades ago. She did not regret a single thing she had done, and she wore the scars with pride. Though she had lost most of the vision in her right eye as a result, lucky that she had not lost the eye itself. Her brother Callain had given her the wounds that had caused the scars, and a promise to return and finish what he had started. It was a myth that all Immortals healed the same, some healed at an exponential rate which left little to no scars, and others lacked that phenomenal healing ability. Though even the weakest immortal healed much faster than humans, they healed much the same.

There was a knock on her door and a wild looking woman with ebony hair entered her room. This woman Frost understood was Daemon's mother and the Empress of the night.

Also the woman who had been taking care of her since Daemon had sent her here to heal and hide. She would also be the Alpha overseeing Frost's Trial of the Cubs, now that Frost was fully recovered and ready to join a pack of her choice.

"Lady Shadow." She said in way of greeting as she bowed deeply to her, Daemon's mother waved her hand in a wave of dismissal.

"Stand Frost, here I am just Shadow and good friend to you." She said lightly, Frost nodded her head in agreement as Shadow gestured towards the door. "Come it is time." Frost followed Daemon's mother out into the village.

Standing outside the drawn out circle for the first trial, Frost watched as the Taskmasters rolled in the boulders that the cubs would be throwing to prove their strength. She was the only female cub present for these trials, and she knew she was not welcome. Most female cubs were not welcome in the trials, though their participation was entirely up to them. This was a male dominated world, the females were given their proper amount of respect as they too could be deadly, but they were looked down upon as the weaker and more vulnerable sex by the males. Typical male behavior Frost thought as she glared up at her larger peers. They jeered down at her and made lewd gestures in her direction. Frost was determined to show them wrong; she was much stronger than they would ever know. She was the last living daughter of Lord Chase De Lune, she was one of the last of a rare breed of pure Lycanthropes. Even if her father had disowned her, she was still of that breed and thus far stronger than she appeared for her small size.

 In fact her small stature was an indication of her breeding, if one knew what they were looking for. So were her blue eyes and her white hair as well. When her name was called Frost stepped into the ring and began to lift and throw the boulders. Sending them sailing across the circle and into the crowd. Until she reached the last and largest stone which she leaned against for a moment before fitting her fingers under the end and began to lift it. No one else yet had even dared to lift the monster of a boulder. Frost lifted it chest high and heaved it to the center of the circle where it landed with a resounding crash. Straightening Frost turned and walked out of the circle her head held high to where the Task Masters were painting the other cubs with the thick blue ceremonial paint across her upper arms and neck.

 For the second trial the Trial of the Hunt. Frost was paired with not only the smallest, but the weakest of the male cubs. This young man was smaller than Frost who was tiny by any standard, and looked like a good stiff gust of wind could blow him over at any moment. Any Immortal was stronger than a human by nearly tenfold, beasts like Daemon or Ayden were exceptions, and they were far stronger. But this Immortal was puny, and weak, she had seen his trial of strength he hadn't even gotten past the second boulder. It was like adding insult to injury, nearly everyone in the village knew Frost was more than half blind in her right eye, but pairing her with this pathetic whelp? What was she supposed to hunt and still keep him alive?

The youth looked down at Frost, like he was the superior of the two. Frost snarled she was not having it that way; she shifted into her lupine form and pounced on the youth thrashing him and making him submit to *her*. When she had him fully submissive to her will, she allowed him to shift and follow her into the woods that bordered the village where they would begin their hunt.

Frost could hear the other cubs in the woods hunting. She growled at her partner and moved deeper into the woods. Seeking large yet easy prey that she could fell with her infirmity as well as keep injuries minimal with her partners obvious lacking in physical prowess, Frost put her nose to the wind and began the hunt in earnest. Using her other senses Frost quickly found an eight point buck and began to hem the beast in. Her partner began to get his attitude back and lunged at the buck prematurely and was gouged severely across the face and chest by the bucks waving antlers as the buck fended them off. Frost approached warily and attacked from the side catching the buck by the throat and dragging it down. She struggled with it before snapping the beast's neck and going to her partner who was whining to himself licking at his wounded chest.

Inspecting him and seeing nothing but superficial damage, Frost snarled at him and snapped her teeth in his face. The youth snarled and snapped back standing and bristling his hackles at her. Frost growled showing her teeth in warning. Her partner rushed her and she was forced to defend and teach him a lesson. When the youth was again submissive to her, Frost shifted back and heaved the deer carcass up and began the trek back to the village.

To be painted victoriously for their Trial of the Hunt in a deep purple paint across their backs. Frost was proud; she and her partner had brought in one of the largest animals of all the cubs kills. To her surprise she saw two familiar faces in the crowd next to the Lady Shadow. Daemon and Ayden were talking comfortably with the Lady Shadow and watching as Frost prepared for the next trial. The Trial of Valor, Frost fully expected her opponent to be the pathetic whelp that she had been paired with in the Trial of the Hunt. When she was called into the circle she was not surprised to see the youth standing opposite her with a wide eager grin on his face. She supposed he was going to try and make her submit to him now. Frost smiled to herself, she was not going to let that happen.

    She was going to prove to this entire pack that she was fit to live despite her infirmity, that she was useful to a pack. That she was fit to join any pack that she chose. It had only been three decades since she had been exiled, but she was going to show the entire Immortal world just how far she was going to go. She was going to rise to a better position in life then her father could have given her, and she was going to become someone important in this world by whatever means was necessary.

    The youth roared at Frost charging at her recklessly, Frost roared in response and attempted to dodge the charge. Only just barely managing to escape the youths clutches because he had been coming at her on her right hand side. The youth stayed on her right hand side where she could not quite see him until he was too close to get away. Trading fierce blows they battled in close quarters as they wrestled for the upper hand. The fight was quickly devolving into an all-out brawl in which only one of them would come out alive. There was no rule against killing your opponent in the trials, though deaths generally did not occur. But in this fight there would be a death, and Frost knew it would be her if she showed any sign of weakness. The youth swept her feet from under her and pinned her to the ground and began beat either side of her head, the harsh blows were stunning. But Frost snarled fighting through the pain and clapped her hands on his head and twisted, snapping his neck before tearing his head from his shoulders for good measure. Spitting the youth's blood from her mouth Frost stood and threw his head down before her. Shocked silence greeted Frost, and many of the faces of the watching crowd were twisted in disbelief. Frost lifted her face and roared a single victorious cry into the night.

After she had been painted in the black ceremonial paint and her face was painted with the white death mask Daemon and Ayden approached her, careful not to approach her on her right side. Even if she viewed them as family that was the one thing they could not do. The one thing Frost would never allow anyone to do. Anyone approaching on that side was liable to end up with more than a few gouges from her claws. Daemon bowed his head in respect to Frost, and Ayden did likewise.

"Lady Frost, it is a pleasure to see you again, I trust my mother has treated you well?" Daemon asked as he walked with her through the village. Frost nodded her head and said lightly.

"Your mother has given me the best care anyone could care to receive, though I do not particularly care for being treated like an invalid." Daemon sighed and motioned with his hand for her to continue. Like he had been expecting her spite about it, Frost was sure Daemon knew well enough that she meant no disrespect to his mother or her pack. Still though she felt the need to explain further. "The

Lady Shadow has treated me with nothing but excellence, but I have long been waiting to prove my worth despite my infirmity, I cannot do that if I am not allowed to do anything on my own." Daemon nodded in response and cocked his head to the side looking to Ayden.

"Perhaps it is time you come to stay with me, there are many things I can teach you, and many things you can learn to do without the use of your eyes." Daemon stated lightly, Frost bowed low to him and responded hesitantly with a simple.

"I would be honored my Lord." If Daemon was willing to take her under his wing, then she was willing to learn. Though she did not fully trust him or Ayden though the pair of them had been there since the beginning of this mess she was in, a mess she had admittedly created herself. She was curious though as to why Daemon did not simply put her down, ended her misery, as most Alphas would with an individual that was impaired in some manner.

Volume One

Chapter One

Gasping Frost picked herself up from the forest floor with trembling arms from where she had landed when Daemon had tossed her about like a rag doll. Rising shakily to her feet Frost wiped the blood from her lips and snarled angrily in the direction that Daemon's scent was coming from, because she could not see him due mainly to the thick blindfold that was tied around her eyes. Daemon gave a ghostly chuckle and said softly.
"You have to learn to anticipate my actions without the use of your eyes; you have to learn to *feel* everything around you." Frost shifted her bare feet in the soft mossy earth; she could hear Daemon pacing lightly across the forest floor. "Now try again and attack me." Daemon commanded, Frost snarled and complied rushing at the sound of his voice she was quick and agile on her feet, but not quite fast enough it seemed.

Daemon's fist caught her in the ribs, knocking the wind out of her. In a quick series of blows Daemon had her defenseless and on the ground yet again. Frost lay there for a long time unable to move or breathe. She could feel Daemon lean over her and heard him snort softly with distaste.

"Get up Frost do not give up on me yet, because I am not giving up on you." Daemon growled at her. "Prove to me you have got what it takes to be in my pack and I swear to you that I will never turn my back on you and I will protect you." Slowly Frost rolled over and rose to her feet her entire body was trembling from exertion. She was physically and mentally exhausted. But she would continue on as long as Daemon wished her to, she *had* to prove to Daemon that she was worth the effort to keep alive. Daemon stalked off to another part of the clearing they were in.

Frost spat out a mouth full of blood onto the ground. She was torn between her desire to trust Daemon's words, and her wariness of them. After all her brother was out to kill her, and her father had exiled her for doing the right thing instead of protecting her like he should have. That was how Frost saw things.

She closed her eyes behind the blindfold and let her senses envelop her, painting a clear picture for her to see of a small forest clearing with just her and Daemon standing slightly off to the side of the center of the clearing. Frost tried to feel everything that was around her as she approached Daemon, and with some success managed to land a few blows before she was again pinned on her back Daemon's teeth against her throat. Gasping Frost held absolutely still wondering what the powerful man was going to do. With a sigh Daemon leaned back and helped Frost into a sitting position.
"We will stop the sparring here for today, come there is still much to do before the day is done." Daemon said helping Frost to her feet.

Frost followed Daemon's scent and the sound of his light footsteps through the forest back to the cabin that he had brought her to after her coming of age trials. It was only a full day's journey from Daemon's mothers pack. But from the second they had arrived three weeks before Daemon had bound Frost's eyes and made her do everything from menial labor to sparring blindfolded. It was not that she was without improvement; she had improved greatly in learning to function while blind. Learning to walk while blind had been no easy feat and she had to rely heavily on Daemon's instructions, and she found he very rarely led her astray. But she was learning to walk on her own without guidance and steadily improved in her daily life.

One could not expect Frost to learn in the matter of a few weeks that which it took years of living without sight to develop. Daemon was not really expecting her to; he was just pushing her because he knew she could do great things if she put her mind to it. He would never let Frost know it but he thought her to be very courageous to have done what she did and endure what she had to endure with such modesty. And he was beginning to think of her rather fondly, like an elder brother would of a younger sister. It would be a shame to waste the potential he saw in her as well. He could still make use of her skills yet, once she overcame her physical limitations.

The days slipped past for Frost in endless darkness. Her only indication of time was Daemon nudging her awake and leading her out into surrounding forest. Eventually she learned to rise on her own and wait for Daemon outside the cabin, using the sounds of nature awakening outside the cabin as her call to wake. Ayden came by the cabin periodically to report in to Daemon, as he had taken on the majority of Daemon's duties while Daemon stepped aside to train Frost. Frost's steady improvement in her rudimentary skills continued as the days slipped into weeks and the weeks into months.

After four years Frost noticed that her senses were sharpening. Becoming keener than they had ever been, Immortals senses were already on par if not better than most animals. But this was something else entirely, her senses were beginning to take over and compensate for her lack of sight. In her sparing matches with Daemon she began to feel the flow of the way the battle was progressing and was able to begin predicting his movements and thusly defend from them. She was also beginning to counter his attacks with her own.

It took a total of three decades for Frost to master herself without the use of her eyes, in all her forms. Daemon would settle for nothing less than perfection. When Frost could at least stand on equal footing with Daemon when they spared and carryout her daily life flawlessly Daemon declared her competent enough to live without the blindfold. It was night when Daemon undid the blindfold, so as to ease her eyes into things without hurting them. Frost looked around them and the cabin they were in, she knew it by heart, knew where everything was from memory. The ability to see did not change that for her, it just added to her arsenal of heightened senses. Daemon was leaning against the wall nearest the door of the cabin watching her as she took everything in. After a long while he spoke.
"Not many people would have endured what you have with the grace and dignity that you have." Daemon said softly to her, Frost looked up at him and wondered what had brought this on.

Daemon shifted his position slightly and continued. "But this is far from over, you have a choice to make now, do you join me and completely forsake your family or do you try to repair the damage done and get back into their good graces." Frost stiffened at his cold words.

She knew he was right, but she did not want to admit it. She would have to choose what was more important to her. Her family or to continue doing what was right and stopping her brother at all costs. It was a painful decision to make, but it was one that she had to make and soon. Daemon straightened and came off the wall.

"This is your last chance to back out Frost, I have given you the tools you need to survive it is now up to you now to decide how you will use them." He said to her as he walked to the door and stepped outside leaving her alone with her thoughts.

Frost was torn between her loyalty to her family and her morals and doing what she felt was right. No one should be above the law. Was she going to remain loyal to a father that had sent her away, choosing her villainous brother over her? Or was she going to continue to stand up for what she believed in? It seemed a simple choice to make. But it was a hard one, because she would be turning her back on everything she had ever known in order to rise up on her own power. It meant that she would have to put faith and trust in a man that was as unpredictable as a hurricane and just as deadly.

  Frost mulled over her choices, weighing the pros and cons of joining Daemon's pack verses returning to her family to try and be reclaimed. If she returned home she might have a chance of being forgiven now that all this time had passed, if she proved that she could still be loyal to the pack but her safety would not be guaranteed. Her future would be unsecure at best, but would be so much easier. Or if she joined Daemon's pack and completely ostracized herself from her family she was guaranteed a modicum of safety, shelter, and quite possibly a secure future, and this path would be the one that cost her everything and would be the hardest one to bear.

She agonized over her decision for weeks, did she choose Daemon and what was right or did she try to reconcile with her family? What was the right path to take? In the end Frost had to remind herself that it was her morality that had forced her to turn her brother in to Daemon. And it was her morality that ultimately forced her to choose the longer, harder road of joining Daemon's pack. When she had made her decision she left the cabin looking for Daemon, whom she had not seen hide or hair of since he had commanded her to pick a side. His scent was faint in the woods but still easy to follow, to make it easier Frost shifted into her wolf form. Putting her nose to the earth she followed Daemon's scent, keeping a wary eye out for anything else that might be lurking in the woods to prey on a lone wolf.

Frost found Daemon sitting on a fallen tree about five miles from the cabin; he looked down at her and cocked his head to the side. Frost dipped her head to him respectfully before lying down and rolling to her back to show her vulnerable belly in the traditional submissive offering from a pack member to their Alpha when being initiated into the pack. Daemon came off the fallen tree and came walking over to her, with a fanged grin he leaned down and rubbed her belly roughly. This was the Alpha's symbol of acceptance, a symbol of trust and dominance. He stood up and motioned for Frost to follow him as he began trotting through the trees, Frost rolled to her feet and swiftly followed after him.

  Daemon led the way through the woods back to the cabin where he doused the fire in the hearth and made ready for their departure. When he returned he had stripped to the waist and was barefoot. Frost was in awe of the sheer solid mass of him, she knew Daemon was a large man, though he was nowhere near as large as Ayden. Then he began his shift taking the form of a huge wolf with raven black fur. Frost bowed her head to him again as Daemon rose to his feet panting from the effort the change had taken. He shook out his fur and lifted his face to the sky and howled. It was a long aching cry that sounded unbearably lonely. Frost lifted her face and added her voice to the melody before Daemon took the first steps into the woods.

They ran for weeks tirelessly through the forest, they passed a small human town that was nestled just inside the forests border and they continued to run. It amazed Frost the changes that had come over the land in the sixty years that passed since she had been exiled from her father's pack. Thin metal tracks crossed the ground in front of them, Frost briefly reviewed her knowledge of the last few years and all the conversations that she had listened to and participated in with Daemon and Ayden, the descriptions they had given her of the wondrous things going on in the outside world gave her all the knowledge she needed to know that these were railroad tracks and they crossed the land like long winding scars linking human cities and settlements, with steam engines carrying goods and arms across the land. Daemon led Frost over several tracks and onward across the Great Plains towards the coast. It took them a few months but they eventually came to a place that Frost came to realize was Daemon's estate.

They entered the grounds through a light forest that bordered the back property Daemon led her right up the back steps and into the house. A thin whip like man was there to greet them.

"Crown Prince Daemon your father sent me to see if you had returned home yet." The man said, Frost pointedly looked away as the sound of snapping bones began from Daemon's direction. After a while Daemon said.

"You may tell my father that I have returned and I will resume my full responsibilities from this day forth, Kain." The man bowed to Daemon and left them alone. Daemon touched the top of Frosts head. "Come let me show you where you will be resting your head for now." Daemon said walking away and down a long hallway, he stopped at the end of the hallway and opened a door for her.

"I will send for Martin in the morning, he is the man who tailors my clothes, I will see that he creates you some appropriate attire for this era." Daemon said as Frost walked into the room, ignoring his nakedness. She did not want to think of this man in that manner, for her he was not mate material. He was too ruthless and far too confident in himself.

Daemon closed the door behind her and Frost heard him walk away. Frost shifted back to her human state slowly, groaning as her bones snapped and reformed. She walked about the unfamiliar room and sighed as she fell into the bed. Sleep was slow in coming but when it came Frost welcomed it.

Volume One

Chapter Two

    Frost slept fitfully and woke with the rising sun, she was pacing in her room covered by a thin robe that was somewhat huge on her she had found in the wardrobe when there was a knock at her door. When she opened it Daemon was standing outside dressed simply, but finely. Next to him was a tall and thin man, who had the smell of a Vampire around him. She assumed that this was Martin so she bowed her head to both of them out of respect and stepped aside so they could enter her room. Daemon stepped back and allowed Martin to enter first. Martin entered and looked Frost over with a pleased smile.
"How my Lord would you like her dressed?" Martin asked looking to Daemon. Who looked to Frost for a long moment as if measuring her mood before he spoke.
"I want her in clothes fit for a high noble Lady; she begins her training as a Royal Knight today." Daemon said coldly as he looked back to Martin.

"Other than that dress her in whatever she wishes." Martin returned his gaze to her.
"My, my, I see you are going to high places sweetheart." He said as he came over to her, he held his hand out to her and Frost took it hesitantly. She did not know this strange man, but something about him was very relaxing to be around. "Now tell me exactly what you're looking for and I'll make it for you." He said as he kissed the back of her hand softly.

After hours of standing still being measured and re-measured Frost was given a pair of leather pants and a linen tunic that would fit someone of her size. When she was dressed she bowed to Martin and left the room. Running into Daemon just outside her door he beckoned to her and she followed him through the manor to a neat little study on the third floor of the manor. Daemon took a seat behind a sprawling mahogany desk, and gestured for her to take a seat. When she had seated herself Daemon began to speak his thunderous voice echoing through the room and Frost's ears.

"Normally at this time I would send you off to the Academy to complete your training, but considering your eye the Academy will not take you, therefore I must train you myself." Daemon said slowly making sure that she understood his every word. "I will not have time to see to you personally all the time as I have done these last three decades, and your training will be a little different from that of a traditional Knight." Daemon folded his hands carefully and looked her dead in the eye.

"Therefore I have arranged for the best instructors in the Empire to come and assist me in training you." Daemon continued lightly. "I trust you will give them the same respect you would give me if I was to train you personally, I will naturally check in on you from time to time and see how you are doing." Frost bowed her head in acknowledgement. She knew that she was getting a priceless gift.

A formal Immortal education was more than she had ever dreamed of, let alone a position as high as the one that Daemon was placing her in.

"Thank you my Lord." Frost stated as she stood. Daemon bowed his head to her and said.

"Your first lesson begins in the grand ball room with Madame Porter; she will be instructing you in all things regarding the Immortal races." He motioned to the side and Kain stepped forward. Frost flinched she hadn't even noticed him enter the room even with all her heightened senses. "Kain will show you the way." Frost stood and bowed to Daemon before following Kain out the door and to the grand ball room.

    Her lessons with Madame Porter were long and complicated. Much more in depth than the basic history lessons that most cadets were given at the Academy. And her lessons with Madame Porter were not just all about history, there were lessons in arithmetic, the sciences, theology, and mythology. The lessons were not just complicated they were challenging, Frost struggled to complete the curriculum assigned to her in the designated amount of time. Madame Porter's lessons took up the first half of the day, the other half Frost was training hard under the sever eyes of Kain in the art of stealth and assassination.

Daemon could find no better instructor to teach her than the man who had been a renowned assassin in his mortal life, who had then perfected his craft as an Immortal, Kain was indeed a very frightening man. Slowly as she was being trained Frost realized that she was being groomed to be something more than a simple Royal Knight or pack noble.

The time flew for Frost; she hardly noticed its passing. She became accustomed to attending parties at Daemon's side in elegant dresses. As the time passed Frost persevered in her studies and training. Becoming sharp of mind and capable of complete and utter silence when she moved, Frost actually had to make an effort to make noise so as to not unsettle people. She was a Lady of the high Courts and had an education to match. Her training had become part of her daily life, a part of her so completely that she needed no weapon. She was the weapon. And like that it seemed in the blink of an eye another thirty years passed her by and

Daemon was knighting her before the noble Courts as his Knight Commander.

The world had changed again and automobiles charged down the streets of the ever-growing mortal cities, telephones were being put in every home, and telephone lines were being run across the land from city to city and town to town. Radios blared the news about a growing human civil war that was happening all around them. Planes roared overhead in tactical formations. Frost watched it all from Daemon's back porch sitting in her wolf form as Kain and Daemon discussed the potential of the conflict spilling over into the coastal city that Daemon's manor and a great majority of his businesses resided in.

The majority of the fighting was taking place over the lower half of the Great Plains from what the radio was telling. Though some of the war had spilled into neighboring cities and towns, the war had as of yet to reach the coast. It was at that moment in time that Ayden strolled through the door, he bowed his head to Daemon, and nodded to Frost. He had popped in every so often over the last thirty years and they had grown close. As their situations with Daemon were somewhat similar, Ayden too felt like he had been groomed to stand in the position that he held and openly admitted it with a wide triumphant smile on his face.

    Daemon turned to Ayden with a pleased smile as Ayden placed a stack of papers on the table beside Daemon before saying.
"I found him my Lord, I found Callain, and the bastard was hiding in plain sight the whole time." Daemon looked shocked for a moment before he started flipping through the papers on the table.
"This report says there are thirty two other Lycanthropes with him, all of them very young do you know where they came from?" Daemon asked softly, his voice rumbling like thunder. Ayden bowed his head sadly.
"They are his pack, his turned children my Lord." Ayden stated slowly, Frost stood up and yipped in anger as Daemon looked up from the papers with a thunderous look on his face.

"And what do your agents think he has gathered these pups to do for him?" Daemon asked in a low growl. Ayden looked up and said carefully. "One of my agents was able to get close enough to one of Callain's gatherings to hear a bit of their plans." Ayden stated carefully before continuing. "Callain is planning on returning to his family home for his sister, even if he has to kill everyone in the compound." Frost growled and shook her head angrily baring her fangs so they glinted in the sunlight.

Being in her wolf form she could not physically voice her protest but she made sure that she was heard. Daemon held his hand out to calm her.
"When did you receive this news?" Daemon asked softly. Ayden sighed and shook his head. "Three days ago when I was in Harjest City, it will take at least two weeks to reach the Immortal City by car, longer if we run." Ayden stated, Daemon looked at the report and sighed. "And Callain was last reported in Gyrsville, that's a small town not even a hundred miles from the rugged mountains that hide Coelum,

he would be there long before us." Daemon said before looking at Frost. Who immediately stood from where she was crouching and came to him, nudging his hand with her snout. "If we go we must go expecting no less than a massacre." Daemon stated. Frost nodded and slipped into the mansion running flat out to her room to get ready.

    Shifting back to her human form Frost dressed in a pair of pants and a tunic and packed her bags. Her heart was hammering in her chest and there was a knot of tangled feelings in her gut. She had pushed her thoughts about her exile to the side since she had been accepted into Daemon's pack; she had abandoned that life completely. But when she thought about it her father's betrayal still stung, the scars there were still deep. She still loved her family dearly and the thought of them in danger scared her to no end. Frost lifted her canvas bag and slung it over her shoulder, she slid a long knife into the sheath at her left thigh, and a pistol into the holster on her right hip. Guns were not much use against Immortals, yes getting hit by a searing hot piece of metal hurt. Frost should know Daemon had made an example of her by shooting her in the thigh during a sparring session, showing her there was really nothing to be feared from being hit by a small caliber bullet.

Most Immortals simply healed to fast to be bothered by the bullet unless they were hit in the head or heart, even then the bullet had to be a large caliber. She did not resent Daemon for doing so; Frost understood that was the way Daemon did things. It was all or nothing with Daemon. Frost held nothing against Daemon for it, she actually held him in high regard for treating her as he would treat any of his other Knights. Personally she thought Daemon had done it out of his form of brotherly love for her. They had grown quite close, to Frost Daemon was her brother and so was Ayden. That was the way Frost personally came to view him over the time that she spent with him. Daemon was a stern and harsh yet kind elder brother who constantly looked out for her and Ayden. They were more than just a pack, more than just fellow Knights; they were their own little close knit family.

    Meeting Daemon and Ayden in the main hall of the manor, Frost set down her bag and surveyed them, noting how similarly they were dressed. Only Daemon was dressed in his official regalia, with a heavy looking sword in his hands. Daemon led the way out the door and to the waiting car. He let Ayden drive sitting in the back seat looking like a King, while Frost sat up front with Ayden watching the world roll by. Ayden pushed the car to its upmost speed as they drove the long paved highways across the land. They only paused to fill the gas tank and relieve themselves. Still it took them the promised two weeks to reach the beginnings of the dirt road that led to the Immortal City. Throughout it all it was a long silent drive with only the radio playing. Frost was anxious, wondering what kind of reaction her father was going to have to her being there if he was even still alive when they arrived. She hoped that he still was, whatever he had done to her, he did not deserve to die.

Volume One

Chapter Three

As the car rolled up to the Immortal city Frost looked at it in awe, it remained as majestic and timeless as it ever had. Upon entering the city the car radio stopped working completely emitting just a soft static buzzing noise. Immortals in the street stopped and stared as the car drove through the cobbled streets and to the gates of Frosts family home. There was already a large crowd outside the gates being held back by Knights of the Royal Guard who looked weary and some who looked rather pale. Ayden climbed out of the car first and opened the door for Daemon who stepped out tying his sword to his belt. Frost stepped out of the car and flanked Daemon along with Ayden and they made their way towards the crowd with a confident stride. The crowd parted before them, many with bowed heads as they saw Daemon, fear in their eyes as they looked upon him. Frost was awed by the reaction that Daemon inspired in the Immortal people, she had grown up hearing stories of his feats from her father. But had not dared to believe there was much truth behind the words. Then there were the looks of fearful awe that followed Ayden, who strode alongside Daemon with such confidence it seemed that it was only natural that he was right there beside the mighty man. Then there was Frost who to strode alongside Daemon with as much confidence as she could muster, the majority of the looks she inspired was wary admiration and plain jealousy. For what woman could make it to be able to stand beside the Lord Daemon's side? The answer was one hell of a woman that was for sure with a sizeable set of fortitude to match.

    The Knights bowed out of Daemon's way and opened the gates for him to enter. Frost hesitated slightly under that wrought iron arch before passing through and falling back into step with Daemon. The courtyard was a mess, blood stained the paving stones and was painted up the exterior walls of the mansion. Daemon was right this had been a massacre and she hadn't even seen the inside of the mansion.

Frost could not bear to look at the neat rows of white covered lumps that lined the west wall of the court yard. She did not want to look yet. Daemon led the way into the mansion and they walked through the rooms, walking through new scenes of destruction and carnage with every step. All the bodies had been removed from the mansion, but the blood remained and in most places it was still wet and thick. Daemon saved the study Frost's father worked out of for last, he and Ayden did not enter.

Hesitantly Frost pushed aside the sundered door and stepped into the room, her father's books littered the floor, pages torn and blood stained. Whereas the in the rest of the mansion the scents had been to co-mingled to make out Frost could make out two distinct scents in this room. Frost could detect her father's light and fresh woodsy scent and her brother's fetid stench. Of the two her father's scent was the strongest meaning the majority of the blood that was pooled on the books and floor belonged to her father. Frost searched through the room carefully and found what she was

Volume One

looking for, a chest buried under the remains of the broken desk. The lock was unbroken and the wood virtually unharmed. Frost carried it out of the room, knowing it held her father's most important documents.

    She handed the chest to Ayden and made her way out of the mansion and into the courtyard. Following her nose she found the shrouded lump that was her father. Kneeling she uncovered him slowly, growling through the cloying smell of death and through her tears as she beheld him. Despite what he had done to her she still loved him, she could not escape that. He looked the same as how she remembered him, closely cropped white blonde hair, and pale skin, paler now in death, short, though taller than her. Frost leaned forward and kissed her father's forehead muttering a blessing for him. Before going to his hand, looking not for his signet ring, Callain would have taken that seeing it as his. But for his Pairing ring, it was a unique ring and something her father had made himself. The face of the ring is what made it so special, the coat of arms on it was her father's personal coat of arms, but it was also a key. The key to the small chest that Ayden was currently holding, the only key.

Frost found the ring on her father's left hand right where it had always been, Callain had never seen the importance of it. But their father had shown Frost when she was young where he kept his documents and how to open the chest. Because she had been disowned she did not have the right to open the chest, so she presented the ring to Daemon. Who bowed his head to her and opened the chest carefully, Daemon pulled out a rolled scroll and began reading it carefully. When he was done he put the scroll back in the chest closed the lid, picked the chest up and placed it in Frost's arms. He held up her father's ring before her eyes and said.
"As of right now you are the sole heir to all your fathers' estates, his fortunes, and his businesses." Daemon handed her the ring. "In that chest is sixty-four years' worth of letters addressed to you, and one very specific last will and testament." He walked away leaving Frost

Volume One

standing there stunned. Ayden came to help her, taking the chest from her and tucking it under one arm he took her hand with his free hand and lead her towards the gate after Daemon. Daemon turned to her as he climbed into the car and said.

"Tend to the burial of your family for now; get your affairs in order when you are ready we will talk about your first assignment." Daemon shut the door and Ayden bowed to Frost handing her back the chest saying lightly.

"Good luck little sister." Frost smiled numbly at him as he jogged around the car to the driver's side and climbed in and drove away.

    Over the course of the next several weeks Frost held several back to back funerals, raising pyres and letting her family and her father's pack burn like Immortal tradition dictated, then entombing the ashes in the packs mausoleum. Her entire family, the entire pack, nearly three hundred Immortals in all, all slaughtered. All of them Frost knew personally and had to bury. The loss that cut the deepest was the loss of her father, yes he had betrayed her, but she still loved him dearly just the same. It took her a while after the funerals to bring herself to read her father's will, and was shocked by what she read.

    Within the will was an official declaration reclaiming Frost as his daughter, and disowning Callain, it was sealed not only with her father's seal, but with the seal of the Emperor's Justice. The Immortal responsible for keeping record of all official records in the Empire, the person whom recorded deaths, births and all things legally binding. This made the will in the eyes of Immortal law beyond just a ceremonial document. Her father obviously had not wanted anyone to contest this.

    In the end Frost sold each of her father's estates and for no small amount either, each estate was worth millions. She put the money she inherited from her father in a new mortal bank account and added the money from the sales from all her father's estates, all seventy two of them. Taking over her father's businesses was no easy feat either; she eventually sold the set of businesses for a hefty sum. It was not that she was not capable of running the corporation; it was not for nothing that Daemon had driven discipline into her head. Constantly driving into Frost's mind that the law must be up held but with reason and discipline, this gave her the rationality to deal with anything in a calm and composed manner, and the discipline to maintain it.

It took her a total of three years to get all her affairs in order, when all the properties and businesses were sold, her family and her father's pack had properly been entombed, and she had been reinstated as the sole heiress of her father's legacy. Reading her father's letters to her had been a heart wrenching experience to say the least of it, and a new fire burned in the pit of her belly to revenge herself upon Callain for taking away her entire family from her. Especially when their father had been so close to reconciling with her, perhaps that was the reason their father had died, but it made no difference now. Frost was going to find Callain there was going to be no rest for Callain until she did and put him in the ground herself. She would find him, no matter the cost. Frost returned to Daemon's side a determined soldier with a new purpose.

    Daemon welcomed her back into his home with open arms, and allowed her to get settled in before summoning her to him to give her the first assignment she would ever complete for him. Frost only brought two things with her from the Immortal City, her father's chest which held all the letters he had ever wrote her and his will, and the canvas bag in which all her clothes were in. On her finger was her father's pairing ring which she had sized and fitted to the first finger of her left hand. She had read and reread those letters a thousand times but it did not lessen the sense of betrayal that she felt in her gut.

    When Daemon summoned her Frost went willingly to his study. She bowed to him as she entered and nodded in respect to Ayden, his constant presence in her life and his constant unwavering determination to show her kindness had eventually won her over. She still thought of him as a big goofy idiot, though she would never say that out loud. Daemon was standing behind his desk looking out his study window; he casually looked over his shoulder at her and raised his hand in a dismissive manner.

Frost rose from her bow and went to stand beside Ayden who was leaning calmly against Daemon's desk. They remained like that in comfortable silence for a stretch of time before Daemon began to speak.

"I am sure that by now you are aware that I have been grooming you to fit a specific roll in this grand scheme of things." Daemon said coolly. Frost did not respond, she knew of course, she had always known that Daemon was training her for more than her mere survival alone. He was preparing her for something more. What it was Frost could never truly know, but she was determined to be ready for whatever Daemon's commands were to be. "As you know the world is changing before our very eyes, mankind has never been more dangerous than they are now." Daemon continued in his cool business voice. "Secrecy has never been our law, but never have we flaunted ourselves to the mortals as Callain has been doing for the last century." Daemon said slowly, he turned around so that he was face to face with Frost and Ayden. "For the last century or so Ayden has been in charge of hunting Callain and we have not gotten close to the bastard." Frost shifted her weight uneasily understanding where this was going and dreading the order that was forthcoming. Daemon put his hands on his desk and leaned forward before growling.

"Therefore I will leave the hunting of him to you; you will have my full resources at your disposal including one extra resource I created once I gained the position of Regent." Daemon stated leaning back and picking up a sheaf of paper from his desk. "You have heard of the Hunter family's before? I am their grandfather and master and they too are looking for Callain." Frost started in shock her eyes widening in awe. She had grown up with stories of the hunters, fiercely dedicated humans that were highly trained and knew no fear. No one knew when, where, or how the hunters had started. They had just started killing Immortals out of the blue and exposing the Immortal to be a criminal in some way.

The humans always left their evidence at the scene and disappeared without a trace. But Frost knew now how the hunters had gotten their start, Daemon had indeed been busy as Regent. She bowed her head to Daemon in acceptance of her assignment, though the weight of it weighed heavily on her. As she turned to leave Daemon said in a gentle manner.
"Of any of us here I believe that only you have the right to kill Callain." Daemon stated softly. Frost paused with her hand on the doorknob of the study door. She knew Callain had taken Ayden's mortal family from him. But Callain had taken everything from her, everything she had ever cared about in this world had been ripped from her by her own brother.

Volume One

Chapter Four

Daemon spent some time preparing Frost for her time in the mortal cities. Showing her how he ran his businesses, as she would be taking over management of some of them as part of her cover. Secrecy was not the law, but it was advised. Mortals were dangerous and with the changing of the times unpredictable at best. Frost was a quick learner and adapted to managing his businesses almost effortlessly when she arrived in the coastal city of Lume, which was an hour drive from Daemon's estate.

This is where the majority of Daemon's businesses and properties were located as it was the capital city of the human government that 'ruled' the great northern continent. In the eight years it took for Frost to master Daemon's strict business procedure and the laws of the human society that she was entering. Frost underwent a change; she had looked upon most males as competition, as essentially her equals. She had fought to prove her worth in the Trial of the Cubs, to prove she was as good as any man.

Now Frost looked down on most men, with the exception of Daemon and Ayden, she viewed them as equals. Her attitude change was because of how she was treated while she was under Daemon's tutelage. The men she had encountered had treated her as less than them, and they weren't even Immortal. These were human men, powerful human men, but mortal all the same. It was the same treatment she had faced at the Trial of the Cubs, it was the same treatment she faced in the noble Courts. It was on the same degrading level of disrespect that she had been shown all her life. After having been betrayed by her father, after having her brother swear to hunt her down and kill her for doing what was right, after having everything ripped from her. Being disrespected by a mortal was the last straw on her already thin patience with men.

Frost did not just strive to prove herself to Daemon in running his businesses or in her task in hunting down her brother. She strove to dominate and subjugate every obstinate male in her path along the way. Frost went out of her way to teach men who showed any form of disrespect to a woman a lesson they would never forget.

As Frost took over the management over several of Daemon's bars and clubs at the turn of the century, just as cell phones, colored television and personal computers were coming into huge production. Ayden in turn took over several others and their paths crossed constantly. As the years passed Frost rose steadily in the night life industry, though she never wavered from her true purpose sending out all her available resources across the land in search of her brother and completing other assignments.

Reports came in daily, but there was no sign of Callain anywhere. Not a hide or hair of him could be found in any city in the north, so Frost sent her people south where they had more luck. But they only encountered whispers of Callain in any mortal or Immortal city in the south. Also in this time she made a name for herself in the human world and the Immortal world, putting herself out like bait to lure Callain out of hiding. It was a dangerous gamble but if it worked it worked. Ten years passed this way and Frost was growing nervous.

Since the murder of her family and her father's pack Callain had disappeared, simply vanished. She knew from past experience that if Callain did not want to be found, he never would be. It was pointless try, but look she must and if by chance she flushed him out of whatever hole he was hiding in then all the better for her. And she was hanging her hopes on her desperate gamble of offering herself up as live bait by making a name for herself in the human and Immortal worlds, by flaunting her success in Callain's face she would bring the wolf to the table.

Frost entered the club with a confident stride, her heels clicking against the floor sharply. She was going to interview a new employee this day, a new male employee. Making her way up to her office she sat behind her desk and pulled the file for the new employee towards her. The picture on the file was of a young man with warm brown eyes and dark brown hair. The young man had a thin and fragile look to him though the picture portrayed him with a wide and handsome smile. Frost read through the file calmly, she liked his references and his work experience was not bad. There was a knock at the door and Frost looked up before saying.

"Enter." She watched as the young man from the file walked into her office with a nervous smile on his face. He walked with a slight limp though his eyes flashed green with the changing of the light, signifying that he was a Lycanthrope of some kind.

Therefore he was Immortal, and with no doubt in her mind knew who she was; the young man bowed his head to her in respect before taking the seat that Frost gestured for him to take. Frost looked him over; she did not get the overwhelming desire to dominate this male, or the urge to subjugate him. This young man had a delicate feel to him and an almost feminine aura about him. Frost almost immediately liked him; she liked him even more as he spoke, because he spoke to her with respect and manners.

"Good evening Lady Frost, I am Jayden Bleu, I am here to request a position as a member of your staff at this club." He said softly, brushing his hair out of his face. Frost took in his manner of dress and was again impressed. Jayden was dressed in a button down tunic, tie, and vest combination that looked dashing on him. Frost looked again at his file and sighed, she really wished she could hire him, but sadly she did not have room for another worker.

    That was when she noticed the bruises that peeked out from underneath his collar. She guessed that Jayden had a partner that was not quite gentle with him. Still she could not take on another employee, but she knew someone who could. Ayden was ever expanding Daemon's business Empire, he could use another good employee, and it might just save Jayden's life she thought as she closed Jayden's file.

"Sadly Jayden I cannot take on another employee at this moment, but I do know someone who is always looking for new employees." Frost said lightly writing the information down on a slip of paper for Jayden. "It might take some time but I am sure that he will take you on." She watched Jayden bow his way out of the office with a tight smile on his face.

Frost picked up her phone and dialed Ayden. She made arrangements with him to make sure that Jayden got hired on the spot. Ayden sounded amused to hear her doing a favor for a male, but Frost knew she would hate herself if anything more were to happen to Jayden because he did not have a place to escape. She had seen through those warm brown eyes and that smile and seen pain and loneliness, almost the same pain and loneliness that she saw in Ayden's eyes whenever she looked at him. Satisfied that she had done what she could for Jayden Frost returned to the business at hand.

Chapter Five

Frost growled as she read a report from one of the Hunter clans from across the land. Callain had resurfaced and he was not alone. He was headed straight for Lume on a killing spree, and all Frost could do was wait for him. This had been part of her plan, she had made enough of a name for herself now that should bring the wolf to the table. She was after all nothing but a helpless half blind female. Where ever Callain had done his hiding he had obviously not gotten any of the Immortal news or he was choosing to ignore the fact that she had been made a Royal Knight.

Daemon was already in the city, and Ayden never strayed far from her side. They were keeping true to their promise to protect her. She was part of their pack; her safety was of utmost concern to Daemon. Though he had been the one that had decreed that she would be hunting her brother, he never said that she had to take him on alone.

Focusing on running her clubs profitably and efficiently Frost kept to her schedule, to her routine. She refused to deviate from what she had set for herself. Naturally Frost knew that remaining in a set routine was dangerous, her brother could easily learn of it, undermine it and her security and deal with her from there. Daemon and Ayden both advised against it, adamantly so. But Frost refused to listen to their pleas. Instead she remained on constant alert for any sign of her brother or the Immortals he was traveling with, his pack. Daemon's agents and Hunters had given accurate descriptions and provided pictures of the individuals that Callain was traveling with. So Frost was not going to be caught completely unawares by her brother.

However Frost did expect her brother to come at her with some degree of stealth and secrecy. He would lay low in the city for a while after arriving and ferret her out. Learn her habits, which people were around her, and what kind of glory or fame killing her and her associates would bring him and his pack. Only then would he dare strike at her. And Frost was determined that she would be prepared for him when he came for her. Whether he came for her at her home or at one of her clubs, she would be ready for Callain when he came for her.

Exhausted Frost returned to her small one room suite apartment, she had said good night to Ayden and Daemon on the floor below hers before retiring to her room. She lay awake for hours staring at the high vaulted ceiling of her room. As confident as she pretended to be in front of Ayden and Daemon, Frost was scared. She knew her brother was coming and she knew how he was going to come for her. But it was the when that scared her; it was the many if's that scared her. Daemon and Ayden were phenomenal fighters but even they could be overwhelmed, Frost was a great warrior but could she hope to compare to her brother? Frost had worked for everything she had gained since being exiled, but her brother had been naturally talented from birth. The arts of war, hunting and violence came as naturally to Callain as breathing.

For her it had never been so easy, kindness and compassion had ever been a part of her even to this day though it was a weakness that she could ill afford. Frost may have gained a level head, she may have gained one hell of a go hard or die trying attitude. But at her core she was still a compassionate person, she may be a little scared and a bit more wary. But compassion was in her nature and that was not going to change. As Frost lay awake long into the night thinking about it, she knew without a doubt that her compassion was what was going to cost her dearly in the coming battle with her brother.

When morning came it found Frost up and ready to greet the day, she had not slept a wink. Not one single second the whole night, that was okay though it was not the first time she had gone without sleep. When she was training with Daemon and Kain she had gone weeks without sleep, she was trained to cope with this. She could handle this with little difficulty. Frost met Daemon and Ayden down in the lobby of the building and they took a sleek sedan to work together, Ayden managing his clubs from his cell phone. Daemon followed Frost to the office and took over the desk as Frost filed the paperwork for the club. It was dawning into the digital age but Daemon preferred that the clubs have paper and digital copies of all their files.

    Frost was more than willing to follow this directive though it made much more work by far for her and the other managers of the clubs. Daemon made a few executive decisions while he was up in the office with her before heading out onto the floor to survey the club scene.

    This went on for a number of months, Frost honestly lost track of the number of them. Time hardly mattered to Immortals, particularly Immortals that were more concerned with keeping their lives. She still managed her clubs effortlessly and flawlessly, but she was more concerned with the never ending span of time that seemed to increase without any word of Callain. All agents and Hunters under Daemon's control lost their leads on Callain two or three cities away from Lume, and that was a worrisome amount of time ago.

Callain could very well be in the city by now and watching her every move. Frost was edgy though she did not show it. She joked with Ayden, conversed normally with Daemon and ran her clubs like there was nothing out of the ordinary. There was nothing Frost wanted to do more than run and hide at that moment, but she could not she was Daemon's Knight Commander, a part of his pack. She had to stand firm beside him and carry out her orders.

It was during one of the long sleepless nights that Frost answered her apartment door and found Daemon standing outside it. He looked at her with a sad look in his eyes as she invited him into her home. He took a seat on one of the small stools that she had in the tiny living space. And Frost sat across from him wondering what brought on this visit. Daemon ran his hands through his hair and sighed.

"When I told you to find your brother, I did not expect you to take this route." Daemon stated slowly, he put his hands on his knees and leaned forward. "You put yourself out there like a piece of bait on a string, I did not offer for you to manage my businesses so you could do that." Daemon stated with a growl. Frost bowed her head to him and bore with the scolding quietly knowing Daemon was not yet finished speaking and thus it was not wise to speak.

"But I must commend your bravery on putting yourself out there like that, it was a very dangerous risk to take and most likely the reason Callain crawled out of his hole." Daemon said after a long pause. He sighed again and tilted his head to the side as Frost looked up at him in shock she had expected a further scolding, not praise. "But I must warn you now Frost, Ayden and I may not be able to get through Callain's pack in time to get between you and him." Frost sighed and bowed her head again.

"I do not expect you to do anything of the sort for me my Lord, Callain is my brother therefore I should deal with him on my own." Frost stated calmly though her heart was pounding in her chest from fright. Daemon looked at her with a tight frown on his face.

"I am your Alpha Frost, I am bound to protect you by the bond we share, but this is even more than that Callain has broken the most basic of our laws and I as Regent must bring him down to enforce those laws." Daemon said softly, "This is so much more than a family feud, you are my Knight Commander, if you strike Callain down it must be done in the name of the law and not in vengeance." Frost looked up at Daemon with awe. In that one instant he had brought back to the fore every second of training he had ever given her, every word he had ever spoken to her. Every time he had drilled into her head the importance of the law.

This was about much more than a family feud, Callain had broken a slew of laws and it was not just her life she should be worrying about. As Daemon's Knight Commander it was her duty to bring Callain to Daemon for judgment, to kill him if necessary, but ultimately to bring Callain to Daemon. Unless Daemon gave her a direct order to kill him on sight. Daemon reached over and grasped her hand.

"I do not understand how hard it will be for you facing your brother; I will never understand how hard it will be for you because killing comes easy to me though I do not enjoy it." Daemon said softly, his voice barely above a whisper. "But if you find yourself with the upper hand over Callain and you think you can do it, sweetheart you do it, you end him right then, right there." Daemon stood and Frost walked him out the door his words echoing in her head.

    Daemon's words and actions gave her a little confusion, on one hand he was reminding her to uphold the law, on the other he had just given her the go ahead to end her brother's life if she was given the chance and had the gumption necessary to carry the deed out. No questions asked, was it because her brother had caused so much grief and she was a Royal Knight therefore she was in an apt position to dispense the needed justice upon him because Callain was without a doubt going to come after her himself? Or was it because Daemon was using his influence to give her a chance to avenge her family and take care of his duties at the same time? Whatever the reason Frost was determined she would do everything in her power to live up to Daemon's expectations.

Volume One

Chapter Six

  Frost went to work with Daemon and Ayden right on her heels. She proceeded to work diligently and efficiently. Through it all she kept her mind off what was surely to come should Callain come barging through her club doors. Over the course of the day Frost went through the list of her clubs as scheduled, keeping to that tight schedule that she had maintained since she had begun working as Daemon's business manager. As the day grew old Frost found herself feeling more insecure, more nervous and on edge. It was like waiting on the precipice of a cliff above a raging sea while a storm threatened to break above you. The thrill of it had her heart racing but her nerves raw from the anticipation of that storm breaking to throw her off the edge of the cliff and into the sea.

  It was the last club of the night and nothing yet had happened. The music was pounding out of the speakers, and the mortals moved violently to the beat of the music. Their excitement and mingling emotions making the very air seem electrified. Like one more spark would set the whole place into a frenzied blaze.

She was out walking the dance floor when the first terrified scream broke over the thrashing of the music. There was a moment of confused looking around, then another scream broke out only to be swiftly silenced. The staff rushed into the crowd to the sources of the screams and then all hell broke loose as close to fifty Immortals, tall and strong men one and all. They began sweeping paths of carnage through the tightly packed crowd as they went. Panic ensued mortals tried to flee whichever way they could and Frost was caught somewhere between the middle of the dance floor and Daemon. Ayden got dragged away by the press of the crowd. He could have easily broken through, but Daemon would want as few human casualties as possible.

It was easier to go with the flow than to fight through the crowd with his size, he would have killed quite a few mortals without realizing it. For Frost it was a different matter altogether, she was both smaller and more nimble than Ayden and could more easily maneuver through the crowd and make her way to Daemon. Who was battling a knot of Immortals that Frost recognized in the steady flashes of the strobe lights as members of Callain's pack. They were pressed so tight together that Daemon could not get a fix on any single one of them at once, he was too busy fending all of them off.

    The dance floor was in chaos, screams echoed in over the pounding music as blood sprayed the walls and coated the floor. Callain's attack was perfectly executed causing the maximum amount of chaos and mayhem amongst the partying mortals. Frost's Immortal staff went down quickly but not without a fight, several of Callain's men died in the process of eliminating them. Nearly twenty in total, but they just kept coming. Frost searched the dance floor for any sign of Ayden, but could not find him in the press of human bodies as they pressed in around her franticly trying to find a way out. It was a slaughter, humans were dropping like flies and Daemon's angry roar could be heard above the noise as he battled fiercely with a thick tangle of Callain's pack.

    Frost caught sight of Ayden then, she watched him being shoved into the basement and the heavy reinforced steel door being slammed shut on him and barred from the outside. She could hear his muffled angry roars echoing from the depths of the club. Frost turned her attention back to Daemon her eye catching sight of Callain sneaking up behind Daemon blade in hand. The steel flashed eerily in the strobe lights and Frost cried out in warning but it was to no avail, Daemon turned to face the new threat only to receive the blade to the chest. Frost could not tell from this distance if Callain had struck a fatal blow, but Callain and Daemon were breast to breast, then Daemon was falling, first to his knees, then forward and to the side. She rushed forward to catch Daemon before his head hit the blood stained ground.

    Callain looked down at her as the scene of massacre slowed down around them. He smiled down at her with a wide and friendly smile.

"Hello dear sister, long have I desired to see you again." He said lightly, his face painted brightly in the blood of his victims, the flashing of the strobe lights giving him a hideous appearance. Frost laid Daemon's head down gently on the blood soaked floor, she could not hear the beating of his heart over the thundering of her own. As scared as she had been before of this day, she was deadly calm now, she knew what she had to do. The same thing drove her now that drove her the day she had decided to turn her brother into Daemon. Callain was a monster she could see that, she had known that from the beginning, she had just been blinded by family ties. She was not so blinded now.

Standing slowly Frost stood to face her brother, the man who had taken everything from her. She bowed her head to him out of respect for what he had once been to her and spoke. "Hello brother it has indeed been a long time, and I have long awaited the day that I would see you again so I could bring you down for what you have done." She declared as she shifted her form into her glorious half form and howled as she charged at him. Callain deftly dodged her attack and slashed her across the back with his sword. He was playing with her, toying with her as he was enjoying this twisted little reunion.

Frost came at Callain with all the skill that she could muster and then some. Through it all Callain taunted her trying to get a rise out of her. Trying to get her on the path to vengeance and off the path of rationality, if it had been years ago it might have worked. But in the back of her mind Daemon's words were pounding in her head, his constant reminders that the law must come before anything else. She did growl and snarl at him and give him plenty of openings to slash and stab at her, drawing him into the illusion that she was on a wild rampage of rage. It was nearly impossible to keep her composure, to remain calm when faced with Callain in the flesh after all that he had done to her. After all that he had taken. But she allowed the complete rationality of her training take over, she stepped fully into her role as Daemon's Knight Commander.

There was no longer any room in her heart for fear, guilt or even compassion for what her brother had become. Both Ayden and Daemon were down for the count. It was up to Frost to end this, even if she died trying. She had to get the best of Callain and somehow get to Daemon and make sure he was even still alive. As she could not even hear his heart beat over the noise of her own fight, the rest of the room was deadly quiet except for the screeching metal of the basement door where Ayden was struggling to get out.

It was a precise and deadly dance that Callain and Frost danced, each of them struggling to gain the upper hand over the other and bring the other down. Somehow Frost had disarmed Callain of his sword, but she was bearing many wounds and her white fur was matted crimson with blood. Callain to had shifted his form, and his tawny hide to was covered in wounds and blood flowed freely from them. Frost's hard earned skill matched Callain's effortless talent, he had slipped up on his training, but he was still a powerful fighter.

Callain's claws sliced her from hip to hip and Frost howled, her fangs bearing down on Callain and tearing into his arm, once she had a hold of him she did not let go for any reason. Latching on with her strong jaws and raking with her claws. No matter how Callain beat her Frost did not let go, his claws shredded her arms and he tried to pry her jaws apart but shredded his hands on her teeth. Frost gripped Callain by the ear and pulled his head down and let go of her grip on his arm only to get a fix on the back of his neck. She was going for the kill.

They struggled for many long moments before Callain let out a panicked cry that summoned his previously distracted pack to his aid. They left their mortal victims to aid their Alpha and fell on Frost just as there was a tremendous screech and a terrifying roar. Frost went down in a hail of fists and claws, still she refused to release her grip on the back of Callain's neck she was determined to tear his head off if it was the last thing that she ever did. She was like a bull dog with a bone, she did not let go. Several hands grabbed her muzzle and started pulling her jaws apart. Allowing Callain to slip free of her grasp as her jaw broke and Frost howled as the pack continued to beat her as their Alpha crawled away, severely wounded but still very clearly alive.

It was at that moment that Ayden crashed into the pack. Killing six of the pack in just as many seconds, transformed into his terrible half form roaring terrifyingly as he came on like a raging black god. Each swipe that his great hands took caved in the skulls of at least two of Callain's pack mates and knocked over three more. They quickly scattered before him and Ayden dragged Frost back behind him, she shifted back to her human form and growled as she crawled back towards Daemon who was lying in a spreading pool of his own blood. Her right leg, and jaw was broken, as were several of her fingers and ribs.

She was covered in gashes and bruises. Upon reaching Daemon Frost rolled him over and pulled his tunic out of the way. Hearing Callain's voice from the door way she looked up.

Volume One

"I'll be back for you sister, this is far from over!" Callain cried as he fled with the remainder of his pack into the night, leaving nothing but blood and bodies in their wake. Ayden came over to them and knelt beside Daemon and inspected the wound in Daemon's chest. Now that the club was silent they could hear the faint beating of Daemon's heart. It seemed that the blade had just missed Daemon's heart. But it was still quite a serious wound, Ayden cradled Daemon's head in his arm, supporting him carefully like he would an precious infant. Before biting into his own wrist, making the wound quite deep, so that it would continue to bleed.
"Open his mouth." Ayden ordered calmly, Frost did not even hesitate. After being with Daemon for so long and being raised knowing what he was. She thought this was an appropriate course of action for Ayden to follow. Ayden pressed his wrist to Daemon's mouth and waited tilting Daemon's head so that he did not choke.

    It took a long while for Daemon to start drinking on his own and when he did Ayden went stiff and his face went pale, sweat beading on his forehead. Somehow it was now Daemon supporting Ayden as his heart beat suddenly sped up then dropped to a crawl and his eyes rolled back into his head and he went limp. There was a long pause before Daemon detached himself with a look of utter disgust and fury. Frost had never seen such fury in Daemon's eyes before as he laid Ayden down gently. He turned to Frost breathing slowly, the wound in his chest was all but gone as were all the other wounds on his body. Without speaking he leaned over her and assessed the damage that had been done to her. He set her broken leg and jaw causing Frost to cry out and Frost heard him muttering under his breath about Ayden being a stupid git. Daemon moved Ayden and then set about looking for survivors. Not a single person besides themselves had made it out of the massacre alive. Callain had come into the club with close to fifty men, and had left with closer to ten, but had managed to kill twenty Immortals, and nearly a hundred mortals. Frost looked around her at the devastation and was sick. This is what her brother had become, what he was turning others into. He had to be stopped, whatever the cost.

"Where do we go from here?" Frost asked almost in despair. Looking down at her from where he stood, Daemon smiled at her reassuringly baring his fangs. He said calmly in a matter of fact voice.

"We hunt him down and we kill him."

Daemon searched through the pockets of Callain's pack mates that had fallen and been left behind. He found a wallet and a slip of folded up paper. Further search of the wallet revealed that the contents held a county ID from some Podunk town up north on the border of the Great Northern Woods, and the folded up paper was a midterm report card. That gave them where Callain was holed up, how he was hiding in plain sight, and where he was recruiting his pack members. Frost looked up at Daemon from the evidence in her hands and gave him a pained smile. They at least had a heading to follow now. Daemon walked back over to Ayden and nudged him awake. Ayden rose to his feet groggily, Daemon came back to Frost and lifted her into his arms. Heading for the door Ayden following behind unsteadily. Daemon placed Frost in the back of his car and Ayden climbed into the passenger seat.

    He started the car and pulled away from the curb while dialing a number on his phone. Speaking quickly in the guttural Immortal language Daemon gave instructions for the cleaning and processing of the club. Several hours later they were nestled in Daemon's apartment recovering and planning their next move. They would need various documents, credentials, written statements, etc. Frost listened intently to Daemon's plan on how he was going to approach the situation with Callain. They were going to infiltrate the human town that Callain was setting up shop at, and they were going to bring down Callain and his pack from there. Frost shivered with excitement and nervousness. Callain better beware because she was coming for him.

Volume One

Artharthian Lore

Arthartha is a land ruled by 'immortals' Or beings who come quite close to being truly immortal. They are strong, fast, and deadly to encounter. There are two main types of Immortal described in the Immortal series. Lycan's and Vampires. As for the Ancients and how they came to be. No one but Vladimir Daemon Mac Tire knows. However it is speculated that the Ancients were once mortals whom survived the first sundering of the world. Remnants of mankind before the sundering.

The sundering of the world.

The sundering is said to be what happened when mankind waged a total global war and destroyed the earth in the process. Through their own innovation and advanced technologies at the time. Many humans made it through the Ages of Waste, but soon forgot their advanced technologies. It is said that mankind designed human's into weapons for their wars. But the sundering happened before these new 'soldiers' could be used. The ancients are said to be the descendants of those engineered soldiers. And while mankind spiraled down into darkness the ancients rose up to claim dominion over the earth. Creating their own peoples and waging wars with each other over the scant resources of the humans they fed upon.

How Lycans and Vampires came to be...

In the long wars that followed between the ancient kings and queens who ruled after the sundering. Two new races came into being. Created by the ancients to become their foot soldiers. Lycans were created first of the two. The ancient forest dwelling kings and queens learned they could give their blood to an animal and then the animal would take on a human form. They were strong and fast, fiercely loyal to the core. Vampires came soon after, an ancient gave their blood to a human and that human became the first of the vampires. They thirsted for blood and were the fairest of the created creatures by the ancients. Vampires were ambitious and could blend well with mortals. Making them wonderful spies and assassins.

Lycan races...

The lycan race is varied, since the 'breed' of the lycan is dependent upon their souls. Their true natures. A lycan can be of any breed of animal, both domestic and wild. Even creatures that have not walked this earth since the first ages of man. The color of a lycan's pelt reflects their personality. The more natural the pelt's color in comparison to the equivalent animal they shift into. Indicates their true natures. As does their eyes. If their eyes remain a natural color to their animal and similar to the eye color of their human forms. Then the Lycan is true and pure. Yellow eyes often indicate a feral nature if the lycan's human eye color is different. Feral or rogue Lycans are more likely to break the laws of Arthartha than others.

Vampires...

Like Lycan's there are several 'breeds' of Vampire out in the world. But since they are of such a secretive bunch. There are only a few breeds that are known well enough at the moment to be listed.

Hale Vampires- Usually the ones that are turned by any other vampire or a born vampire. They are often robust and healthy, their sires often chose to turn the particular human. Either because they cannot bear or sire children of their own with their mate. Sometimes Hale vampires are created by accident. These members of immortal society are often bribed or paid off by their sires to leave them alone.

Lesgate Vampires- True blooded vampires whom cannot go out into the sunlight. They are loners and hate other people, and absolutely loath Lycans. These particular vampires are believed to be extinct.

Sanguinus Omarus- A sub classification for a particular breed of vampire. Also known as a Sanguine Vampire. They are usually recognized by their pale skin and violently red eyes. Sanguine Vampires are thought to have extraordinary reproductive capabilities. The males are capable of conceiving children and giving birth. Sanguinus Omarus is the sub classification of the Nolucturn Sanguinus. A powerful race of vampires who are reclusive and highly secretive.

Made in the USA
Columbia, SC
09 February 2021